The Pity Party

8th Grade in the Life of Me, Cass

The Pity Party

8th Grade in the Life of Me, Cass

ALISON POLLET

ORCHARD BOOKS
AN IMPRINT OF SCHOLASTIC INC.
NEW YORK

Lyrics from "I'm Sticking with You" by Lou Reed, 1969
Published by John Cale Music, Inc.

LIBRARY OF CONGRESS CATALOGING-IN-PUBLICATION DATA
Pollet, Alison.
The pity party : 8th grade in the life of me, Cass / by Alison Pollet.
— 1st ed.
p.   cm.   Sequel to: Nobody was here.
Summary: When Cass Levin, an orphaned eighth-grader at Elston Prep
in New York City, begins a friendship with Rod Punkin, her world begins
to change.
ISBN 0-439-68194-4
[1. Orphans — Fiction. 2. Traffic accidents — Fiction. 3. Grief —
Fiction. 4. Friendship — Fiction. 5. Preparatory schools — Fiction.
6. Schools — Fiction. 7. New York (N.Y.) — Fiction.] I. Title: Pity
Party : eighth grade in the life of me, Cass. II. Title.
PZ7.P7586Pi   2005   [Fic]—dc22   2004022331

10 9 8 7 6 5 4 3 2 1   05 06 07 08 09

Printed in the U.S.A.   23   First edition, July 2005
Text type set in 11-point Hoefler Text. Display type set in Circus Dog.
Book design by Marijka Kostiw

Thank you,
Amy Betz,
Charlotte Sheedy,
and — as always
— Lawrence King.

Saw you hanging from a tree,

And I made believe it was me.

I'm sticking with you

'Cause I'm made out of glue.

Anything that you might do,

I'm gonna do, too. . . .

THE VELVET UNDERGROUND

ELSTON PREPARATORY SCHOOL
8th GRADE ENGLISH — MS. GLITCH, 4th PERIOD
READING LIST

In addition to your grammar textbook and your
<u>Norton Reader</u>, you will need to purchase the
following books at the Elston Prep Bookstore.

PHAN →

<u>JANE EYRE</u>
BY CHARLOTTE BRONTË

<u>OLIVER TWIST</u> ← orphan
BY CHARLES DICKENS

okay, not about orphans, but NO MOM!

<u>TO KILL A MOCKINGBIRD</u> ←
BY HARPER LEE

<u>THE ADVENTURES OF</u>
<u>HUCKLEBERRY FINN</u> ← *YOU'VE GOTTA BE KIDDING ME!!!*
BY MARK TWAIN

WILLIAM SHAKESPEARE'S
<u>A MIDSUMMER NIGHT'S DREAM</u> ← *gotta be an orphan in there*

EDITH HAMILTON'S ← *ORPHANS X A ZILLION*
<u>GREEK MYTHOLOGY</u>

<u>THE MEMBER OF THE WEDDING</u> ← *OH, PUHLEAZZZE!*
BY CARSON McCULLERS
IS THIS A JOKE OR WHAT??????????

Chapter One

Cass Levin was in her bedroom, on the top floor of the town house, when she heard the familiar sounds — the wheels of the cart scraping the sidewalk and squeaking to a stop, then footsteps on the stoop.

Cass stubbed her toe and nearly broke her neck tearing down the stairs. She swung open the front door with such force that she startled the mailman, who nearly fell backward. They stood blinking at each other for several moments, Cass's eyes adjusting to the bright outside. The first thing she saw clearly was the packet of mail in his hand — the yellow envelope was on top.

"Finally!" she yelped, swiping it away. She'd shut the door halfway when she realized how rude she'd been, then poked her head back out. "Thank you!" she cried cheerily, hoping it didn't sound like an afterthought. The mailman was already backing his cart down the stoop.

Back upstairs, Cass made a beeline for the telephone to call her two best friends. "Well, what are you waiting for?" she whooped, when they said their class schedules had come, too. "Get over here — pronto!"

Penelope and Tillie lived on opposite sides of Manhattan yet somehow managed to arrive at the same exact moment. Cass's eyebrows rose suspiciously when she opened the door to see her friends standing side by side. "We made a pact! If you guys opened them without me, I'm going to go ballistic!"

Tillie was a pale girl, who was allergic to just about everything on the planet as well as the sun. "Nice to see you, too," she said drily, barging past Cass to get inside the house, tossing off the visor and jacket her mother had made her wear.

Penelope remained outside, grinding the tip of her sneaker into the front step. She'd gotten braces the day before, and her gnawed bottom lip jutted out poutily. "Oh, what, you're mad?" Cass balked. Penelope held up her envelope, still sealed. "I was just joking!" Cass tried not to sound as impatient as she felt. "I know you wouldn't do that. Sheesh!"

"Three, two, one . . ."

"Ouch!"

Opening the envelope, Cass got a paper cut. It was whisker-thin and shaped like a frown and stretched across the tip of her index finger. A drop of blood dribbled onto the letter from the principal, landing on the sentence "Welcome back, middle schoolers, to

Elston Prep, recently ranked New York City's finest private school."

"Okay, is everyone ready?" Tillie asked, glancing first at her own schedule. "Anyone have first-period French?"

"I do!" hooted Penelope.

"Nope," said Cass.

"English with Mr. Linzer?"

"Same," Penelope gasped.

"Uh-uh." Cass shook her head.

"Third-period Geometry?"

"Me, too!" said Penelope.

It kept going like this. Until Penelope and Tillie had every class with each other. And Cass had every class by herself. The room was silent but for the *ssss* sound of Penelope sucking air through her new braces.

Cass was a tall girl, who'd returned from summer camp even taller. She stretched her legs out, feeling like they didn't belong to her. She didn't have to look up to know that Penelope and Tillie were staring. She could practically feel their eyes boring into her forehead — horrible sorry-for-you eyes. There was nothing Cass hated more. "Sheesh," she groaned, concentrating on her kneecaps, "it's just a stupid schedule. Quit it with the pity party."

Cass was used to people feeling sorry for her, of course. Her parents had died in a car accident when she was eight years old. "A tragic car accident," it was usually called. That was shorthand for "it wasn't just a fender bender — people were hurt, and not just moderately but *tragically*."

Tell people your parents are dead, and it's always the same. After the "I'm sorry's" and the "How horrible's," they run out of things to say. That's when the looks start. They gaze at you with woeful eyes, frowning to show you how sorry they feel, then scrounge for something to nervously fiddle with — a packet of Sweet'N Low at a restaurant or a pen on a desk, looking far too happy when the topic finally changes and — *phew!* — they're free. What a relief to be out from under the dark shadow of Cass's dead parents!

Cass hated people feeling sorry for her, and she hated the looks, so they were all the worse when they came from her two best friends.

She sucked on her wounded finger, feeling like all the energy had been sucked out of her.

Chapter Two

Over the weekend, Cass wallowed in her bad luck. Maybe she didn't like people to feel sorry for her. But feeling sorry for herself was another matter. How could it be that she had no classes with either friend!? And did they have to have *all* their classes together? She rejected Penelope's invitation to lie out on her roof, preferring to spend the last day of summer vacation holed up in her room watching an Alfred Hitchcock movie marathon. She went to bed with a head full of scary movies and a stomach full of Chinese takeout, feeling like a giant lump.

But something odd happened on the morning of the first day of school; Cass awoke feeling strangely invigorated. She popped out of bed before the alarm clock even buzzed. The bad mood was still there, only now there was an electric quality to it — it zipped from limb to limb, until Cass's entire body whirred with the injustice that had been done to her. She felt like a windup toy that had been too tightly wound! Cass tore through her closet, threw on her clothes, then crammed her feet into her sneakers, tripping on the laces on her way down the stairs.

7

A song she'd learned at summer camp was going through her head. It wasn't at all how she felt, but she sang it at the top of her lungs. "OH, HOW I HATE TO GET UP IN THE MORNING! OH, HOW I HATE TO GET OUT OF BED!" Those were the only verses she knew, so she sang them over and over again, stopping when she arrived at the breakfast table to find her guardian, Bea Levin.

It wasn't a coincidence that Bea and Cass shared a last name. For a very short time, many years ago, Bea was married to Cass's grandfather, who'd died before Cass was born. When her parents had been alive, they'd talked about Bea as being "so much younger" than Cass's grandfather. Now it was hard for Cass to imagine Bea as younger than anybody.

"Well, someone's full of pluck this morning!" Bea remarked from behind the arts section of the newspaper. Cass couldn't see her mouth, but she could tell from the crinkles around Bea's eyes that she was grinning. Cass shrugged, flopping into her seat.

Bea favored clothes that resembled pajamas, and pajamas that resembled clothes. As she rose to fix Cass's breakfast, the bottom of her draping silk gown dragged along the tiled floor. This was a beckoning call for Sylvia Hempel, a shaggy mutt with a catlike fondness for pouncing on moving objects. "Looks

8

like everyone's punchy this morning!" Bea laughed, shaking the dog off. "What'll it be, my darling, pumpernickel rye or pumpernickel raisin? Eggs coddled or poached? And, no, Ms. Hempel, I'm not talking to you!"

Cass waited for her breakfast, drumming her fingers on the table, thinking about how she liked the word "punchy": It meant "energetic," but it made her think of cartoon characters bonking each other over the head. Cass's dad had been a writer who'd loved making lists of interesting words — funny ones like "flimflam," "smirch," and "hullabaloo" were his favorites. Cass had inherited this habit; now she made a mental note to add "punchy" to her word list.

Like most students at Elston, Cass lived on Manhattan's Upper East Side. But unlike her classmates, who resided in the gargantuan apartment buildings looming over Park Avenue, she lived in a town house farther east and slightly south. This made her the first one on the school bus every morning — and the last one dropped off.

Usually, Cass resented having a longer ride than everyone else. But, today, stepping onto the bus, the endless rows of yet-to-be-scuffed vinyl seats seemed to tell her what she'd already been thinking: "You're on your own, kid! It's you against the world!" She chose the window seat on the right-hand side of the last row.

"Sure that's the seat you want?" the bus driver asked. Cass nodded into the rearview mirror. "Okay," he said, shaking his head, "but you're asking for a bumpy ride."

"Rad glasses."

"Check out the shades!"

"Nice glasses."

Cass didn't know what had possessed her to put on the sunglasses. She certainly hadn't meant to bring them to school; she couldn't even say how they got into the side pocket of her overalls. But when the school bus hit a pothole, sending the glasses flying from her pocket, it was only a matter of moments before they found their way onto her face.

Cass's sunglasses were plastic with heart-shaped frames, the kind sold on street corners throughout the city. Except Cass's were vintage from the 1960s, maybe earlier, even — they were so vintage, the plastic was scratched, and they were missing a lens. She'd found them in a desk drawer in her room — Bea said they weren't hers; where they came from, she couldn't fathom.

Cass was too levelheaded to believe in magic — *magically enhanced sunglasses, please!* — but there was something about wearing these that made her feel powerful. Impervious, too. That was another one of her dad's words. *Impervious: unaffected by other people's opinions.* Yes, that was it! Cass stepped off the bus and onto the gravel driveway, making her first strides onto campus as an eighth grader, shielded by her sunglasses, feeling entirely impervious.

The sunglasses may have called attention to themselves, but they took attention *away* from Cass. So, she didn't mind the comments — the boy who yelled, "What's with the glasses?" or the girl who whispered, "I can't believe she's wearing those." Even the catty remarks gave Cass a boost. What did she care? They were talking about the sunglasses, not her. By the time she got to class, Cass felt more than impervious. She felt invisible, but also invincible. So what if she didn't have classes with her friends?

CASS'S SYNONYMS FOR "ORPHAN"
CHECK YOUR THESAURUS. IT'S TRUE!

Foundling

Guttersnipe

Mud Lark

Ragamuffin

Rustle

Stray

Waif

Urchin

Imp

Scamp

Soul

Thing (Really, It's True.)

Wastrel

Castaway

Castoff

Nestling

Chapter Three

All Cass's life, her favorite subject had been English. But with one glance at the reading list for Ms. Glitch's fourth-period class, she knew that was about to change. Every single book was about an orphan. *Oliver Twist, The Adventures of Huckleberry Finn, Jane Eyre.* Orphan, orphan, orphan! What kind of sicko assigns a million books about orphans?

Cass was mulling this over, when suddenly everyone in the classroom was talking at once. Cass turned her attention away from the reading list and toward the commotion.

Here was something Cass had observed: You could tell a lot about a person based on how she entered a room. Some people (like Penelope) shrunk when they entered a room, but others (like Bea) made a room shrink when they entered it. On the first day of school, most students skidded into class, fidgety and squirrel-eyed: "Am I in the right place? Is this English class?" But Annabella Blumberg, the eighth grade's most popular girl, simply glided in.

Cass wasn't obsessed with Annabella — at least not in the way everyone else was. She didn't care about how pretty Annabella was or what clothes she wore. She definitely didn't want to be friends with her, but she did like watching her — in the way scientists on nature shows observe their subjects, anonymously and from a safe distance.

Annabella didn't look around to see who else was in the class, or double-check her schedule, or even catch a glimpse of the teacher. She sauntered over to a desk and slunk into a chair, as if to say that any place she ended up was the right place to be.

TO PENELOPE
(Open when bored.)
I wish for my sake you were in my English class, but I'm glad for your sake you're not.

#1. This teacher might be psycho.
#2. Guess who's in this class. Yup, LILLIAN LANG and . . .
#3. ANNABELLA DUMB BERG (yes, I know, I'm immature!)

Ms. Glitch had a burbly way of speaking, as if her voice was coming from inside an aquarium instead of the front of a classroom. "Levine, Cass? Are you here? Cass Levine, hello?"

Cass coughed loudly — as if a frog in her throat was what had delayed her response. "Yes, I'm here," she said, "but it's Levin. Cass. Levin." Cass hadn't meant to sound haughty, but she wasn't upset that she did.

Considering the dread she'd invoked in Cass, Ms. Glitch was a surprisingly puny woman. "Oh, dear, my mistake," the teacher warbled apologetically, scribbling a correction in her notebook. "Okay, who's next, let's see . . . Ah, we have a new student. Punkin, Rod? Rod Punkin? Please say I have that right."

The response came from directly behind Cass. "Positively presently present is Punkin, Rod!" barked a boy with the rat-a-tat precision of a machine gun.

There was tittering in the room. "I'll interpret that as 'Here,'" Ms. Glitch replied drily after it died down.

Cass had to see this guy! She whipped her head around. A crazy grin gawped back. Rod Punkin was a spiky-headed boy in a striped T-shirt that was unraveling at the neck. On his desk, facing her, was a piece of loose-leaf paper propped up like a triangle.

HEY LEVIN, NOT LEVINE,
WANT TO GO DOWN THE HILL WITH ME?
MAYBE WE CAN GET DUMB BURGERS. ROD

Next to the word "burgers," he'd drawn a picture of a cheeseburger wearing a dunce cap.

Cass turned back to face the teacher, her head exploding with all the horrible things "Go down the hill with me" might mean. She clapped her notebook shut, then for extra protection, propped her elbows on top of it.

"Now, I know we've got a lot to cover this year," Ms. Glitch was saying, "dangling participles, thesis sentences, split infinitives . . . But that doesn't mean we can't have fun." At the word "fun," Ms. Glitch picked up a copy of the reading list; it drooped in the dull afternoon air. "On this reading list are some of my absolute all-time favorite books."

Some of your favorite books about orphans, Cass thought crossly. *What does "go down the hill" mean?*

"We're going to read them. We're going to write about them. We're going to talk about them. And that brings me to the first order of the day." Ms. Glitch sunk to her knees to open a desk drawer, from which she pulled a large hat. "In this hat are numbered pieces of paper," she announced mysteriously. "The number indicates which discussion group you're in." The room crackled with confused murmurs. "That's right, discussion groups. There are four students per group. You'll meet every Friday. I want you to see this as an *opportunity*."

"I want you to see this as my socks-are-hurting-me," rhymed Rod Punkin in a whisper loud enough for only Cass to hear.

"You might think it odd at first," Ms. Glitch warned them. "All I ask is that you try to be open-minded."

"You might think this Rod's the worst. All I ask is that you try not to be blinded."

Cass opened her notebook and scrawled another note to Penelope, this time in extra-gigantic letters, so that someone peeking from behind could see the words loud and clear.

REMIND ME TO TELL YOU
ABOUT THE KID WHO
SITS BEHIND ME IN ENGLISH
CLASS. HE'S A FIRST-RATE
WORLD-CLASS PSYCHO!!!!
WE'RE TALKING SERIOUS
BEHAVIOR PROBLEMS.

Ms. Glitch laid the hat on Lillian Lang's desk. Lillian acted like picking first was a privilege bestowed upon her, rather than a simple consequence of having chosen the first desk in the first row of the classroom. She made a big to-do of rolling up the sleeve of her oxford and showing off a wrist of bangles and woven friendship bracelets, then dipped two fingers, clawlike, into the hat, rummaging around until Ms. Glitch reprimanded her: "Ms. Lang, we don't have all day."

"Mine says number one!" Lillian announced — as if that, too, signified greater meaning.

Cass picked briskly but also got #1. *Please don't mean what I think this means,* she thought.

"This is your chance to get intimate with the material," Ms. Glitch announced once everyone had picked. The word "intimate" sent a current of snickers across the room. "Okay, okay." Ms. Glitch sighed. "Bad choice of words. But that just goes to show you how important choosing your words can be. You'll keep that in mind when putting together your presentations."

The room erupted in a chorus of: "Presentations?"

"What do you mean, presentations?"

It was a well-established fact at Elston Prep that discipline and rigor were the tickets to an Ivy League university, and so unstructured assignments were a source of great panic.

"Are we going to be graded?"

"You know, eighth-grade marks count for college!"

"Each discussion group will make a presentation to the class," Ms. Glitch explained calmly. "This presentation can take any form — a group skit, a song, you can act out a scene from a book in mime, as far as I'm concerned. Just as long as you're creative, just as long as you work together. We'll be starting with *Oliver Twist* by Charles Dickens, and I see no reason why the first group to present shouldn't be number one. Who's in number one?"

Two hands in front of Cass went up — one belonged to Lillian, of course; the other — Cass noticed with a gulp — to Annabella Blumberg. But where was the fourth? She turned her head to the right, the left . . .

"Okay," said Ms. Glitch, making notations in her roll book. "Number one is Lang, Blumberg, Levin *not* Levine." She glanced at Cass and threw her a wink. "And, who's that in the back? Ah, yes, the inimitable Mr. Punkin."

It turned out being #1 was nothing short of doomed!

The bell rang. Someone plunked a note on Cass's desk. It said:

YOU'RE ONE TO TALK ABOUT BEHAVIOR PROBLEMS.

Next to the word "problems" was a drawing of heart-shaped sunglasses that were missing a lens.

Chapter Four

A week into eighth grade, Cass was still wearing her sunglasses around school, though not all the time. Cass treated the glasses the way Wonder Woman treats her magic lasso: If abused, the powers might fade, so they should be used only when absolutely necessary. Lunchtime was one of those times.

"Don't you get a headache wearing those?" Tillie asked, digging a fork into her macaroni and cheese.

"Nope," Cass answered swiftly, then took a giant chomp of her turkey sandwich to indicate Tillie should switch subjects.

Tillie turned to Penelope. "You did the Geometry homework, right? Please say you did. Oh, phew. Cass, you're so lucky you don't have Mr. Lee. The guy is evil."

"Yeah," agreed Penelope. "He's even harder than Bobkin, and I thought *he* was the hardest Math teacher Elston had!"

Cass didn't want to talk about her sunglasses, but she didn't want to talk about Penelope and Tillie's classes, either. She pushed the glasses up the bridge of her nose.

"And what is the deal with Madame Zousis? She doesn't let us speak any English in class. Isn't that crazy? I mean, we don't speak French yet. What language are we going to speak? Chinese?" Penelope chuckled at her own joke, glancing up at Cass expecting she'd join in. She didn't. "Really, though," Penelope finished. "She's such a jerk."

"*Such* a jerk," echoed Tillie.

Cass took out her annoyance on her lunch. The more Penelope and Tillie talked, the quicker she ate. In a matter of minutes, she'd wolfed down her lunch, including the chocolate-chip cookie she'd bought for dessert and the can of Country Time Lemonade she'd mistakenly purchased from the soda machine — she'd meant to push SPRITE.

The conversation swung back to Cass, though she didn't like this subject, either. "So, what about the psycho kid in your English class?" Penelope asked her.

"What psycho kid?" Tillie asked Penelope before Cass could respond.

"Cass wrote me this note about how there's a psycho in her English class."

"Cass, you write Penelope notes during class? You never write me notes! How come?"

Could words get stuck in your teeth? Because if

they could, the words "What does 'go down the hill' mean?" had been stuck in Cass's teeth for the entire first week of school.

"What does he look like? What's his name?" Penelope asked.

"Rod," Cass answered, thinking how funny the name sounded in her voice. "He's got short hair, and he wears gigantic black boots."

"Wait, is his name Rod Punkin?" Tillie asked her. "Because I heard Hope Alder saying he got kicked out of Ancient Civilization for being disruptive, which is pretty amazing because he's new, which means who was he talking to? Himself?"

Cass tried to nudge the words out of her mouth. They stayed put. She imagined them welded to her teeth like Penelope's new braces.

"Maybe he's got a disease. Can you have a disease where you can't stop talking? Cass, maybe you could get him an appointment with Doris." Tillie was referring to Cass's aunt, Doris Blume, who was one of New York City's most prominent psychotherapists.

Spit them out, Cass told herself. *Spit them out. Here I go.* "Hey, and you'll never believe this," she managed to get out. "But, he asked me —"

"Want to go down the hill?"

What in the world? Those were the words Cass had been about to say, but that wasn't her voice!

Cass looked up to see the hovering figure of Lillian Lang, who returned Cass's stunned look with a snarl. "Well, *excuse me* for trying to be friendly! I just wanted to know if you wanted to go down the hill. You know, eighth graders have off-campus eating privileges this year, right?" She looked pleased to see they had no idea what she was talking about. "We can go down the hill — that's what upperclassmen call it. You know, to Burger King or to Vinny's Pizza."

While Penelope and Tillie pretended like they knew what Lillian was talking about, thoughts chugged through Cass's brain: *Elston Prep is on a hill. To get to Burger King, you go down the hill.* A giant laugh surged in her stomach. It came out of her mouth sounding like a honk. *Down the hill. Burgers. Down the hill.* Cass honked again.

"I guess that's a no, Cass!" Lillian sounded offended now. "You know, everyone's always saying you're crazy. I thought you just wanted attention. Why else would you wear those glasses? Now I think they're right."

Cass ignored Lillian. "What was *that* about?" Penelope and Tillie asked once Lillian was gone. "Why were you laughing?" Cass brushed them off, too. She was too busy happily banishing from her brain all the many things she'd thought "go down the hill" might mean.

Ms. Glitch suggested that, as a way to break the ice, they give their discussion groups names. Since their presentation was on *Oliver Twist,* Lillian suggested the Twists, sounding giddy with her own cleverness. No one else cared enough to argue, and then they sat for several moments, not discussing anything.

It was Rod who finally broke the silence. "Do you ever feel like just screaming?" he asked them. "Like what if right now I just stood up, opened my mouth, and screamed?"

Lillian's eyeballs popped, as if they had slingshots behind them.

"What do you mean?" Cass asked him.

"Oh, come on! You never think that?"

"I'm not saying I don't," Cass said, even though she never had thought about screaming like that. *Is there something wrong with me for never thinking about screaming?* she wondered. "I'm asking you to explain."

"Well, sometimes, I'll be somewhere, and I'll just think, 'What's stopping me from screaming at the top of my lungs right now?' Because it'd be so easy to just do it."

"We're supposed to be discussing *Oliver Twist*," Annabella Blumberg reminded them while studying her fingernails.

"I am!" Rod's voice rose insistently. Annabella still didn't look up. "That's my point. Why doesn't Oliver Twist just scream? He's being starved, the other kids are jerks, he has nothing to live for. What's stopping him from letting loose a crazy bloodcurdling scream?" At that, Rod pushed back his chair and gripped the edge of the desk so hard his knuckles turned white. He opened his mouth. . . .

Cass watched in amazement. *Is he really going to do it?* Lillian inched her chair away in horror, making painful squeaks on the linoleum floor. Annabella continued to examine her nails.

"Psych!" Rod laughed when, after several seconds, he closed his mouth without having made a sound. "But see how easy it would be?"

"You're insane," Lillian told him.

"What if I am?" said Rod.

Maybe it was because not long ago Lillian Lang had called *her* crazy. Maybe it was because she herself felt guilty for calling Rod a psycho. Maybe it was because she agreed with the things he was saying. But something in Cass went rushing to Rod's defense. She thought about the part in the book when Oliver Twist gets up in front of everyone in the dining hall and asks for seconds. "In a way, asking for more is Oliver Twist's way of screaming," she said, looking from Lillian to Annabella, then, for a split second, to Rod. "It's pretty nuts, what he does."

"Oliver Twist does *not* scream," Lillian snapped back. "I read the first chapters three times."

Cass tried to be patient. "Oliver doesn't actually scream, Lillian. But when he asks for more gruel, that's like screaming in the way Rod means. It's not like he's going to *get more* because he asks. He *knows* that. But he asks, anyway. He's kind of . . ."

"Crazy," Rod said, finishing Cass's sentence while bugging his eyes out freakishly at Lillian.

Cass flipped open to the part in the book where Oliver asks for more. *"Child as he was, he was desperate with hunger, and reckless with misery."* Cass liked the sound of the phrase "reckless with misery." *"He rose from the table; and advancing to the master, basin and spoon in hand, said: somewhat alarmed at his own temerity: 'Please, sir, I want some more.'"*

"Oliver Twist is *not* crazy," Lillian argued. "He's hungry. Plus, he was a victim of peer pressure. His friends made him do it!" She reminded them how the other kids had forced Oliver to ask for more. "The reader should feel sorry for him." Cass winced at the familiar words. "You think you would have done something differently if you were in his place, hmmmmmm?" She was staring straight at Cass.

Rarely did Cass consider telling someone that she *was* an orphan, but the thought of making Lillian Lang feel ashamed was very appealing.

"I think that's a good question, Lillian." If someone as tiny as Ms. Glitch could loom, the teacher was doing just that. She stood above Cass's chair, which meant her chin was only an inch from Cass's head. Cass slumped in her chair to make more room between them. "I think that's a promising way to explore the choices Charles Dickens made when constructing the beginning of the book. This is wonderful, you guys! I love that you're disagreeing. Put all this energy into your presentation!"

Across the room, Group #2 — who'd been assigned *Jane Eyre* and had renamed themselves Eyre Supply in honor of the band Air Supply — were disagreeing a little too much. "People, people, please!" Ms. Glitch cried.

"I think our presentation should be a play," Lillian announced. Since Annabella's opinion was the only one that mattered, she looked directly at her when she said this.

But Annabella sniffed dismissively. "I hate plays.

All those people up on stage spitting into the air. It's so embarrassing."

Then Cass had an idea. "We could make a movie. My aunt has a video camera she could lend us."

"What kind of movie?" Annabella asked.

"Well, it could be about what would happen to Oliver Twist if he didn't ask for more, if he just screamed instead." Cass was thinking out loud here. She thought about the Hitchcock films she'd watched the day before school started. "Well, maybe it's a horror movie."

"That's sick!" snapped Lillian.

Rod clapped. "Yeah, sickly great."

Annabella took a moment to think. "I'll do it. Just as long as I don't have to get all dirty, and I don't want fake blood on me."

It was decided: They would spend the next few Fridays plotting out the script. Then, the Saturday before their presentation, they'd shoot the film. Cass's house was the most convenient one for everyone to get to — and, anyway, she was the one with the camera.

"Okay, but we'll have to finish early," Lillian informed them, consulting her assignment book. "That's Halloween."

The note arrived on Cass's desk in the form of a paper airplane. It said:

SO WHAT YOU'RE SAYING IS OLIVER TWIST IS A BEHAVIOR PROBLEM, TOO?

This time, Cass turned it over, scribbled quickly on the other side, then sent it back.

yeah. Oliver Twisted.

An accident involving a dangly earring and the zipper on a backpack created a logjam at the class-room door.

"I think you just came up with the title for our movie," said a voice in Cass's ear. Rod sounded like an entirely different person when he whispered.

Chapter Five

Officially, Sylvia Hempel was Cass's dog. But ever since Cass had returned from summer camp, she'd been acting more like Bea's. She slept at the foot of Bea's bed, not Cass's. She followed Bea around the house, not Cass. Cass tried not to take it personally. She knew Sylvia Hempel was punishing her for going away. But wasn't it time the dog got over it? Now Sylvia Hempel wouldn't even let Cass take her for a walk.

"I'm sorry, okay?" Cass told the paw sticking out from under Bea's bed. "You think it was easy for me? I missed you, too!"

The paw didn't move.

"You're only punishing yourself, you know. I'm not the one who has to get walked. What? You're only going to let Bea walk you now? Well, Bea's not going to be home until dinnertime. You think you can hold it in till then?"

Cass had to lie on her side to fit her head all the way under the bed. Two yellow eyes glowed petulantly at her. "C'mon out, silly Syl," Cass said in her most coaxing tone. "Please?" She showed the dog the leash in her hand. "I'll take you on a walk. A really long walk. We can go to Central Park! Oh, and guess who's coming. Penelope and Tillie! You love Penelope and Tillie!"

Finally, with much difficulty, Cass managed to hook the leash onto Sylvia Hempel's collar. Once the dog emerged from under the bed, her stubbornness disappeared. She shook herself out, let loose three maniacal barks, then charged down the stairs, taking Cass flying along with her.

Penelope was climbing the stoop, just as Cass was yanked out the front door.

"Sheesh, Sylvia Hempel, don't be such a jerk!" Cass scolded.

Penelope looked shocked. "I can't believe you just called Sylvia Hempel a jerk."

"Yeah, well, you don't know, she can be one." Cass paused on the front step to catch her breath.

Penelope rubbed Sylvia Hempel's head fondly. "Are you in a bad mood or something?" she asked.

"Are you talking to me or the dog?"

"You!" Penelope said with a laugh.

Cass told her she wasn't, then thought: *Sometimes when someone asks you if you're in a bad mood, it can actually put you in a bad mood.* "Where's Tillie?"

"Oh, she didn't tell you, she has her first bat mitzvah lesson today."

"Hmmmph, I don't know why she's doing that," Cass said. "I know for a fact she doesn't believe in God. Want to go this way?" Cass pointed west, which was where Sylvia Hempel was pulling her, anyway.

"Yeah, well, her mom grew up in this Orthodox Jewish family, and they were really strict. They didn't let girls have bat mitzvahs, only boys. So, she wants Tillie to have the opportunity."

Cass could understand that, but of all the opportunities girls should fight for, the right to be bat mitzvahed wouldn't be on top of her list. To memorize all that Hebrew! And you had to write a speech!

"You sure know a lot about Tillie's mom," she told Penelope. They crossed Third Avenue.

"Well, she told us about it at dinner last night. I was over there studying Geometry — which is *so* hard, by the way! Are you doing triangles? I hate triangles, but I hear circles are harder. Anyway, Tillie's mom ended up cooking for us. She's taking Greek cooking lessons. Have you ever had moussaka? It looked scary, but it tasted really good. That's lamb, you know."

"Yeah," Cass said, even though she hadn't known. "But I think eating lamb is disgusting." She hadn't actually, until this moment, thought this, but something in her told her to take her declaration yet further. "I have a policy: I don't eat baby animals."

Penelope eyed Cass suspiciously. "You ate veal at

my parents' house, remember? You know a veal's a baby cow, right?"

"I made an exception. I didn't want to be rude." Cass didn't give Penelope the chance to question her further. "So, since you know so much about it, what else does Tillie's mom do?" Last year, Tillie's parents had gotten divorced. Ever since, Tillie's mom, Cherry Warner, had been on a mission to "find herself."

Penelope stopped walking. "Wait," she said. "Are you mad I went to dinner at Tillie's house? It wasn't like it was planned," she stammered. "It just happened."

"Why would I be mad?" Cass scoffed, feeling insulted. Did Penelope think she was pathetic enough to be hurt?

"Maybe you think you weren't invited!"

"I didn't think that!" she told Penelope. *Should I think that?* she thought in her head. "Soooooo," she drawled impatiently, stomping ahead. "*What. Else. Does. Tillie's. Mom. Do?*"

Penelope jogged to catch up. "She volunteers at the folk art museum, and takes a bunch of classes, and spends way too much time planning Tillie's bat mitz-vah. That's what Tillie says, at least."

"Why doesn't Tillie tell her to butt out?"

"Even if she did, her mom wouldn't," Penelope replied. "Not all of us are lucky enough to have Bea, you know."

33

"What's that supposed to mean?"

"Oh, come on! You know Bea's not like a regular mom!"

"Maybe because she's not a mom." Cass hadn't meant to make Penelope feel bad, but out of the corner of her eye, she saw her frown.

"You know what I mean. Bea listens to you. She treats you like a person. She'd let you do anything! You have no idea how lucky you are." As someone who'd lost her parents at the age of eight, Cass was probably the opposite of lucky. Still, she thought she knew what Penelope meant.

On Lexington Avenue, Sylvia Hempel jammed her snout into the subway grate and refused to move. "What could be so interesting down there? You're gonna get your big nose stuck!" Cass tugged at the dog's leash. "Oh, great, she has green chewing gum in her beard."

"Poor Sylvia Hempel," cooed Penelope. She bent down to nuzzle the dog's neck. "Ooooh, I think that gum's sour apple flavor." They kept walking. "Can I ask you a question?" she asked, not waiting for Cass to answer. "Do you ever want a boyfriend?"

Penelope had a tendency to say things out of the blue, but this seemed particularly odd to Cass. "Huh?" was the only reply she could muster.

"Don't get mad. I'm just asking. Do you ever want a boyfriend?"

"I don't even think about it," said Cass, because she didn't. "Do you?"

"It's more like I like the idea of having a boyfriend, but I don't like any boys, you know?" Cass watched Penelope's forehead scrunch up in contemplation. They might be best friends, but they were complete opposites in how they thought about things.

If I wanted a boyfriend, I would get a boyfriend, Cass told herself. *I wouldn't waste my time thinking about the idea of having a boyfriend. But, anyway, I don't want a boyfriend. So why am I even thinking about this?*

Cass changed the subject as they entered Central Park. "I heard that if you come here in the middle of the night, there are rats the size of kittens," she told Penelope.

"No way!"

"It's true. They're like this big." She made a space between her hands, the length of a loaf of bread, for a second almost letting go of Sylvia Hempel's leash.

"Once I saw a rat in the middle of West End Avenue eating a bagel!" Penelope said.

"Yeah, well, this friend of Bea's bought a soda at a hot dog stand and there was a dead rat inside the can! Inside the can! He couldn't figure out why the straw wouldn't go down all the way!"

Talking about rats was sport for kids growing up in Manhattan, so Cass and Penelope talked about them for the rest of the walk. As far as Cass was concerned, they made much better conversation than Tillie's mom, bad moods, and imaginary boyfriends.

But talking about rats could make you feel like you were seeing rats. Penelope was positive she saw one dash under the Mister Softee truck, and then Cass could have sworn she saw one riding the carousel. On the way home, she even thought she felt one scurry across her sneaker. But that was just Sylvia Hempel, who'd stepped on Cass's foot in hot pursuit of a bird.

Chapter Six

Bea's voice wound its way from the kitchen down the hall, through the double-parlor room, and up the stairs to Cass's bedroom.

"CASS, WOULD YOU MIND SETTING THE TABLE?"

It was a funny thing about people who lived in town houses: They screamed a lot. Going upstairs to say three words was a lot of effort — especially compared to just opening your mouth. Cass sat at her desk. "HOW MANY ARE WE?" she hollered into her Geometry textbook.

"THREE!" came the reply.

Of course, thought Cass, *three*. It was Monday. Doris came to dinner on Mondays.

"I THOUGHT WE'D EAT IN THE GREEN-HOUSE IF THAT'S OKAY WITH YOU. . . ." Bea yelled. Cass looked over her Geometry assignment one last time before heading downstairs.

Despite some obvious drawbacks — a ladybug in the bread basket, a vine from a hanging plant in your soup — Cass liked eating in the greenhouse, which was more like a room with glass walls than an actual house. It looked out onto the backyard, where Bea kept her sculpture collection — Bea was an art collector, and her sculpture collection was world-renowned.

Buds from an overhead azalea plant wafted onto the table. Cass swept them to the floor with the back of her hand. She put out three plates, three water glasses, two wine glasses, napkins, forks, and knives. They weren't having soup tonight, and since Doris was on a diet, they'd wait until she left to have ice cream. So Cass didn't bother with spoons.

With a booming practice on West End Avenue, and four *New York Times* best sellers to her name, Cass's aunt, Doris Blume, was a Manhattan household name. Soon she'd even have an institute to call her own. In fact, The Doris Blume Institute for Psychoanalytic Training and Treatment was but weeks from opening day.

Doris had a plump beaming face and a deep affection for eye makeup. In the glossy light of the greenhouse, Cass could see that her aunt's eyelashes were caked in turquoise mascara.

"Well, well, well, if it isn't the eighth grader extra-ordinaire!" Doris exclaimed. They sat down at the table.

Clangs came from down the hall. "Dinner's ready! Just one more sec!" Bea called out. "I need to feed the dog."

"Feed the dog, feed *us*!" Doris grumbled, flashing a greedy look at the basket of dinner rolls.

"You can eat one if you're hungry," Cass told her.

"Oh, I'm not *not* eating it to be polite!" Doris snorted at the absurdity of this. "I'm not eating it because it's bread. I'm allowed only one portion of bread a day, and today I already had a bagel and a half. I know, I know, so sue me, I couldn't resist."

"Food, glorious food!" sang Bea, her cheeks ruddy from the steaming platters of food — roasted chicken, buttered couscous, and asparagus vinaigrette. She ladled couscous onto Cass's plate. "One scoop or two? How about two?"

Despite having just eaten dinner, Sylvia Hempel wasted no time foraging for scraps. She shuttled back and forth from Bea to Cass, waiting for one of them to cave — or to at least drop something. She barked as Doris spooned herself some gravy.

"So, what's going on with our Ms. Hempel?" Doris asked. "She's behaving a little neurotically, no?" Doris chewed on an asparagus spear and gazed pensively at the dog. As a psychotherapist, she was very good at looking concerned.

"Bea babies her, that's what's wrong with her," Cass replied staunchly — she reached across the table for a roll, knocking the saltshaker onto the floor, leaving a trail of crumbs and salt in her wake.

"Oh, that's not in the least bit true!" Bea put on a voice that sounded more insulted than she probably was. "Cass, I would have passed the bread basket to you," she added plainly.

Cass, I would have passed the bread basket to you, Cass mimicked in her head.

The tossing of tableware had only encouraged Sylvia Hempel. Cass could feel the dog's hot breath on her leg. Sylvia Hempel's beard was damp with the liquid from the chicken pan that Bea had poured over her kibble. "Oh, sheesh!" Cass groaned, realizing there was still chewing gum stuck in her fur.

Bea mistook Cass's close inspection of Sylvia Hempel as Cass sneaking her table scraps. "Oh, Cass, please, we only encourage her when we indulge her. Plus, she really did eat a ton. It's not healthy."

"I'm not feeding her anything!" Cass scowled, throwing her empty hands in the air as proof. "You're the one who feeds her nonstop, not me!" *The nerve!* Cass shoved a piece of dinner roll in her mouth. It sat drily at the top of her throat.

Doris had been silently observing the exchange. Now she nodded her head several times. "Hmmmmm-mmmmm," she hummed.

"What?" asked Cass. This was one of the problems with having a psychotherapist in the family. *Here we go again,* she thought.

"Well, if you want my professional opinion," said Doris. *What if I don't?* wondered Cass. "Sylvia's being triangulated."

"Oh, Doris, spare me!" Bea said with a snort.

Cass thought "triangulated" sounded violent. Like being strangled with one of those metal triangle instruments they make you play in kindergarten music class. "What does that mean, anyway?"

Doris rattled off the definition, sounding a little like she was on a game show. "Triangulation: Sometimes when two authority figures have a disagreement, they use a third, less powerful person — or animal, as the case may be — to absorb the conflict, who, in turn, may develop a stress disorder, even behavior problems."

"Does that mean I'm an authority figure?" Cass asked with a laugh. *Is Sylvia Hempel a behavior problem, too?* she wondered.

Doris responded to a glare from Bea by waving Cass's question off. "Oh, my brain's mush," she replied, wiping her forehead with the back of her palm. "Let's not get into it now." She glanced at Bea, who was still grimacing. "Anyway, don't we have more important things to discuss? I want to hear about your eighth-grade travails. Spill!"

Bea and Doris liked to hear all the details about life at Elston Prep, the "nitty-gritty" as they called it. Cass told them about the Twists and the movie they'd be making. She had to admit, just talking about it gave her that buzzing feeling. "Well, it's set in an orphanage, obviously. I'm thinking lots of blood. Maybe a hatchet." She glanced at the chicken. "And some orphan will die by carving knife, definitely. Or maybe that's boring. . . ." She thought about this for a second, wondering if someone could die by can opener or saltshaker or maybe a dog's leash. *Ooooh, would that someone be Lillian?* Lost in thought, it took her a while to realize that Bea's and Doris's eyes were zooming into her.

"What? What? What?" Cass sputtered.

"A horror movie?" asked Bea incredulously.

"What's wrong with that? It's creative!" Cass said, because usually Bea complained that Elston Prep didn't encourage its students to be creative enough.

"But it's a little crass, don't you think? Couldn't you write something instead? A story or an essay? You're such a marvelous writer. Remember those wonderful stories you wrote at camp? Now, *they* were terrific. Doris, weren't they terrific?"

"Oh, absolutely. More than terrific. Stupendous."

Cass crashed back into her chair, thinking, *So you want me to be creative — but it has to meet your standard of creativity. Sorry to disappoint you.* A downpour of azalea buds hit her plate, and she grumbled, "Those stories were dumb."

"Oh, now, I take that as a personal insult," said Bea, piling plates on top of the dirty platter. "I thought those stories were magnificent."

"Well, we're making a horror movie," Cass said in her most decided voice. "And, Doris, I said you'd lend us your video camera. Everyone's counting on it, so you have to say yes, okay? Please, please, please!"

Doris looked from Cass's pleading face to the empty bread basket, gazing trancelike at the butter-soaked napkin for several long seconds before following Bea into the kitchen.

Chapter Seven

It was hard for Cass to hear over the clattering of pots and plates.

"A horror movie about orphans! It just sounds so violent. . . ."

"It *is* violent. . . ."

"Well, that's not good!"

"But, Bea, violent things happen in life. Who knows that better than she does?"

"I know, I know, you're right, but still —"

"Better to confront these things than to bury them. . . . Usually, you worry she keeps too much inside."

"I just worry, period."

"Of course you do. That's normal."

"Hatchets!"

"She's got to be angry, Bea. Lord knows she'd have good reason if she were. This could be a good release for her. Look how excited she is."

"I just can't help thinking . . . she's going to be thirteen soon. The teenage years are difficult for anyone, let alone someone who's already been through as much as she has."

"She's a great kid, Bea."

Cass could hear Bea banging the box of Cascade against the counter to get out the lumps. "That isn't the point," she told Doris.

"You said it yourself. It'll only get rougher for her. Grief changes as we age. It's good to know she's got a solid base."

A solid base? It sounded like they were talking about a piece of furniture, not a person, not her!

"I shouldn't have been so dismissive about her film," Bea said sadly.

"You can apologize."

Not so quick, you can't! thought Cass smugly. She was pleased to know Bea felt bad, but she also liked the charge she got from feeling angry while knowing she was right.

"Would you feel better if she started seeing someone again?"

The dishwasher let out an angry grunt, and Cass couldn't hear Bea's answer. It didn't matter; she knew what it would be. By "someone," Doris meant a therapist. Naturally, Bea would feel better if Cass started seeing someone again. *But I would feel worse!* Cass thought defiantly. *I'm not going to feel worse so you can feel better.*

The other day in English class, Ms. Glitch had taught them about the third-person point of view — when a writer refers to a character as "he" or "she."

"The third person puts distance between a writer and her subject," Ms. Glitch had said. Well, Bea and Doris had been talking about Cass in the third person, and — funny — that's just how Cass now felt: distant. Not just from Bea and Doris, but from the person they'd been talking about — the good kid, who was also angry and kept too much inside.

Hearing about yourself in the third person makes you feel like a third of a person! Cass thought, basking momentarily in how clever she thought this sounded. Then, not wanting to hear anything else Bea and Doris had to say, she went up to her room.

Cass's bedroom wasn't technically an attic, but its sloping walls and wood-beamed ceiling made it feel like one. Cass closed the door behind her, wondering why Bea and Doris had to make everything so complicated.

She did her homework at an old-fashioned roll-top desk, the kind with drawers and compartments of all different sizes. If you can tell how old a tree is by counting the rings, it was the same for Cass's desk — only the rings were a chain of chalky stains left from too-hot mugs of cocoa and too-cold cans of Coke.

Opening the bottom drawer made Cass remember something her mother once said. "Isn't it funny how everything in this cupboard simply screams Bea?" She scrounged in her head to place the memory.

We were in the kitchen at the cottage.

Mom was looking for mugs.

She wanted tea.

I was eight.

Cass peered into the drawer and wondered, *Does anything scream Cass?* The desk had been there when she'd moved to Bea's house, and this was the drawer where she'd found the sunglasses. Now it was filled with gnawed-on pencils and stray sheets of stationery. There was her assignment book from seventh grade, three old bus passes. There were buttons she'd inherited from her father, who, in keeping with his love of words and phrases, also liked slogans. WHY BE NORMAL? balked a purple one. BE NICE TO ME begged another. There was a button facing downward, so crusty with rust, just touching it to turn it over stained Cass's finger orange. It said, THE BERKSHIRES ARE FOR LOVERS.

The Berkshires, which was a mountainy part of Massachusetts, was where the cottage had been — down the street from a farm and near a lake, on a street called March Hare Road. Bea had owned the cottage, but that July, she'd gone to Europe, inviting Cass and her parents to move in. "We're cottage-sitting," Cass remembered her mother saying.

It was hot during the day but cold at night; in the mornings, the air was wet. Cass remembered mornings most. Cass's parents, Will and Bess Levin, had both been writers, so they'd spent mornings writing. "Quiet time," they'd called it.

This was how Cass had spent mornings: She ate apple-cider doughnuts; she dunked her feet in the lake; she named the cows, then tried to teach the cows their names — it never worked. She picked poisonous berries off the bushes, then mashed them up for paint. And sometimes she stayed inside and did what she called "investigating" but her father called "rummaging" — as in "You shouldn't be rummaging through Bea's stuff."

But Bea's stuff isn't like other people's stuff! Cass remembered thinking. *Stuff would have to be hidden for me to be rummaging!* Bea kept photographs in cloth-covered boxes arranged like books on a shelf. You couldn't open a drawer without discovering a pile of handwritten letters from friends with funny names, some in languages Cass didn't understand, some in ones she couldn't even identify.

She'd want me to look — I know she would! Cass remembered thinking, though at that point, she hadn't really known Bea well. Unraveling the mystery of Bea became Cass's summer project, and by the end of the summer, she knew all sorts of things: like how Bea always kept three jars of different kinds of honey in the refrigerator. Like how she used lilac perfume and lavender lotion. Like how she knit but never finished anything she started. How else could one account for the garbage bag of one-armed sweaters crammed behind the patio sofa?

Memories could be tricky, though. Because now, knowing what a month later would happen to her parents — it had been July, and by August they were dead — Cass remembered her summer project not as *getting to know Bea* but as *preparing for life with Bea*. As if somehow she'd been easing herself into the change her life was about to take.

Cass slammed the desk drawer shut, as if doing so would turn off the memories in her head. The buttons rattled inside.

Somewhere, somehow, could I have known?

Country sleeping was different from city sleeping. In the apartment Cass had shared with her parents, trucks ground garbage, cabs honked, and bottle rockets popped. At the cottage, the chirping crickets kept her up.

Will Levin may have collected words for fun, but Bess Levin liked connecting them. She was the kind of person who could at any moment come up with a rhyme. Like "falafel" with "waffle." "Jasmine tea" with "come and see." She taught Cass to do it, too. That summer, before bed, Cass and her mother made a game of muffling the crickets. It was a rhyming game — Bess went first, Cass went second.

> *I love you more than Peanut Chews*
> *I love you more than kangaroos*
>
> *I love you more than a bee makes honey*
> *I love you more than jokes are funny*
>
> *I love you more than a book has words*
> *I love you more than a cat hates birds. . . .*

She wouldn't have admitted this to anyone, but sometimes, Cass still put herself to sleep with these rhymes. Lights turned out, eyes shut, curled toward the wall, she recited them. Sometimes she could hear her mother's voice mingling with her own.

> *We could rhyme until the end of time*
> *About the many ways that you're sublime,*
> *But now we have to go to bed*
> *So close your eyes, relax your head.*
> *You'll sleep until it's time to wake*
> *And dream of all the rhymes we'll make.*

The window next to her bed looked out on Bea's sculpture garden, and tonight that's where her dream took her. It was a hazy gray dream, and there were no people in it. Even sculptures of people no longer resembled people. In the dream, they had faces but no expressions. There were sockets where eyes should be, a small hill of clay where lips should go. It was all so eerily smooth, and Cass woke with the odd sense that despite being snug in her bed, she was not where she was supposed to be.

Chapter Eight

For their trips down the hill, Cass, Tillie, and Penelope chose the Hudson Parkway Diner instead of Burger King or the pizza place. That way, they could order grilled cheese sandwiches for lunch and black-and-white cookies for dessert.

Bea had once told Cass that black-and-white cookies were only a New York thing, but Cass refused to believe it. How could the rest of the country survive without the best cookie on earth? Black-and-whites were large and spongy and crisply frosted in two half-moons of chocolate and vanilla. Cass tried to broker a deal with Penelope. "I'll trade you my black half for half your white half!" Penelope declined.

"So, Cantor Luznick says I have to do the entire haftorah portion *and* at least a parashah of the Torah," Tillie told them.

Cass was Jewish, but she'd never been to Hebrew school, and she wasn't getting a bat mitzvah. She asked what a parashah was.

"A paragraph," Tillie told her.

"Also, I have to pick a theme for the party, so you guys need to help. I'm thinking peace or old movies."

Penelope suggested the fifties, but Tillie reminded

her that Vicki Feld was doing that already. Then Cass had such a good idea, she jumped in her seat, banging the table with her knee and sending their hot chocolates sloshing onto saucers. "What about black-and-white cookies?" she asked. "The entire party could be black and white. The tables, your outfit! You could have a giant black-and-white cookie for a cake! And what are those hats the boys have to wear?"

Penelope didn't go to Hebrew school, either, but she knew a little bit more than Cass. "Yarmulkes," she told her.

"Yeah, they could look like black-and-white cookies, too!"

For some reason, Tillie didn't seem as dazzled by Cass's brilliance as Cass was herself. In fact, she completely ignored her suggestion and launched into an entirely different subject. "Okay, let's play a game! If you could invite any boy to my bat mitzvah, who would it be?"

"Huh?" said Cass. She was still thinking about black-and-white cookies, which were obviously so much better than peace!

"I said: If you could —"

"I heard you," Cass told her. "I just don't know what you mean."

Penelope jumped in. "It's a hypothetical question," she explained to Cass. "If Tillie asked me that question, my answer would be . . ." She placed a finger on her lips as if she were thinking really hard. "Ben! The kid who was in my Algebra class last year." Usually, Penelope got flustered when she talked about boys. Now she seemed oddly calm. "So, Cass, who would you invite if you could invite any boy?"

Cass didn't know what kind of game this was, but she didn't like it one bit. "Nathaniel," she answered. Nathaniel was Penelope's younger brother — he was nine. Tillie and Penelope said that didn't count.

"Too late," Cass told them. "That's who I pick." And, anyway, they had class in ten minutes; it was time to go back up the hill.

That afternoon in Geometry class, they reviewed isosceles triangles, which were composed of two lines of equal length and a third unequal one. Staring at the example on the chalkboard, Cass connected the lines in her head and wondered, *Am I the unequal line?*

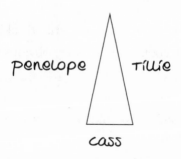

Chapter Nine

"I'm a very patient person, but, Mr. Punkin, you're trying my patience," groaned Ms. Glitch after Rod had talked out of turn for the seventeenth time that day. "You know the rules. I call on you, you talk. Otherwise, zip it. Do you understand?"

Rod made a zipping motion over his mouth.

"This isn't grade school, Mr. Punkin, spare me the shenanigans. And don't think your reputation doesn't precede you! You should appreciate the rare faculty member who doesn't send you to the principal's office every time you act out."

It was October, and Rod Punkin was now the most infamous eighth grader at Elston Prep. "He just blurts stuff out of nowhere!" Cass heard Hope Alder tell Tillie. "No matter when or where!"

"In gym, we were doing rope climbing, and Rod Punkin started cursing," Penelope reported. They were in the cafeteria, so she checked to see if teachers were around. She cupped her hands over her mouth and whispered just in case. "He said the F-word, the S-word. He said words I didn't even know!"

"I heard he was in a mental hospital before this,"

Cass heard Lillian Lang tell Annabella. "And I have *very* reliable sources."

All this may have been true. Still, Rod Punkin was the force driving the Twists. His father was a producer, so Rod knew a lot about making movies, and by October, due mainly to Rod's industriousness, the Twists were set to go. They had a script, they had props, and somehow Lillian had finagled full access to the theater's costume department. "Everything has to be returned exactly as we found it," she told them at least a hundred times.

Annabella had even made a contribution — and a pretty major one, too. "If I'm playing the lead, can't the character be called Olivia Twisted?" she wanted to know. Cass and Rod agreed to tweak the script. Now the movie was *Olivia Twisted* — about the twin sister Oliver Twist never knew he had.

Aside from Rod Punkin, the other popular topic among eighth graders was Timberwood. Timberwood, short for the Timberwood Nature Center for Exercises in Environmental and Interpersonal Relations, was part of the Elston campus, even though it was out in the country, and — according to the Elston Handbook — "a world away from the rigors of the classroom."

Every year, eighth graders visited Timberwood. They went for a week, twenty students at a time, to endure the trials of outdoor life. They slept in wood cabins, cooked their own food. They hiked, they traversed, they even made apple cider. They would return "enriched." Or so the Elston Handbook also said.

For days, rumors had been flying that the Timberwood schedule was about to be posted. No one knew how they'd be dividing the grade. By gym class? In alphabetical order? Cass was hoping they'd be picking at random. *Maybe I'll be put with Penelope, and Tillie will be left out! Or maybe Tillie and I will be in the same group, and Penelope will be left out!* These weren't thoughts she said out loud, of course.

It was rare for Ms. Glitch to end a lecture before the bell rang. "The administration has asked me to make an announcement," she told the class. "It's regarding Timberwood. You'll be pleased to know . . ." Behind her, Cass heard Rod use pencils to play a drum roll on the side of his desk. Ms. Glitch squinted crossly until he stopped. "As I was saying, you'll be pleased to know that, this year, we'll be dividing the grade up by English class."

This time it was Annabella who blurted. "But I don't have any real friends in this class!"

"You'll be going, actually, I should say *we'll* be

going — I'll be joining you as faculty advisor — in April. I think that sounds like a divine time to hit the outdoors, though you know what T. S. Eliot said. Does anyone know what T. S. Eliot said?" No one did. "April is the cruelest month, breeding / Lilacs out of the dead land, mixing / Memory and desire, stirring / Dull roots with spring rain. . . ." The bell interrupted her. "We'll prove T. S. Eliot wrong, class, now, won't we?!"

Penelope and Tillie had a free period, and they were waiting for Cass outside of English class. Apparently, they were in the first group of students going to Timberwood — that meant they'd be leaving in January. "So when are you going?" they asked in unison.

"The first week of April? You can't go in April!" cried Tillie. *Does Tillie already know that April is the cruelest month?* Cass wondered. "That's my bat mitzvah!"

Meanwhile, down the hall, the French teacher, Madame Zousis, was having an even louder outburst. "*Ça suffit, Monsieur Punkin! Ça suffit!*" she was shrieking. Cass turned to see Rod Punkin, grinning sheepishly as he was already being tossed out of French — class had started only a minute ago. Cass herself was running late.

She turned back to her friends, their faces frozen in identical frowns, and for the first time thought, *What would happen if all of a sudden, right now, in the middle of the hall, I just opened my mouth and screamed?*

HAVE YOU EVER WONDERED
WHAT WOULD HAPPEN IF
OLIVER TWIST HAD A TWIN SISTER
WHO WASN'T SO POLITE?
WHO DIDN'T JUST ASK FOR MORE,
BUT SCREAMED FOR MORE . . .
WHO . . . KILLED FOR MORE?

THE TWISTS

IN ASSOCIATION WITH MS. GLITCH'S 4TH PERIOD ENGLISH

PRESENT

A TALE OF BLOOD, GORE, AND MORE

OLIVIA TWISTED

STARRING **ANNABELLA BLUMBERG** AS *THE KILLER*

COSTARRING **LILLIAN LANG** AS *THE VICTIM*

PRODUCED AND DIRECTED BY **CASS LEVIN & ROD PUNKIN**

PLEASE, SIR, I WANT SOME GORE!!!!!!!

RATED TF* BY THE MOTION PICTURE ASSOCIATION OF ELSTON PREP

*TERRIFYINGLY FRIGHTENING

Chapter Ten

Recently, Cass had been losing things. In the past month, she'd lost her pencil case, she'd lost her Ancient Civ book, she'd lost her bus pass.

It was early in the morning on the day of the film shoot, and Cass couldn't find her sunglasses. "WHERE IN THE WORLD CAN THEY BE?" she shouted at the ceiling. She unzipped her backpack, then turned it upside down, shaking it until everything fell out. The floorboards in Cass's bedroom sloped in the middle — now pens and pencils rolled every which way. A cherry LifeSaver, linty from the bottom of Cass's backpack, slid under the desk chair.

Bea had heard Cass shriek. Now she stood in the doorway, panting from the climb, covered in flour and parmesan shreds — Bea had been baking cheese pennies. "Oh, phew, you're okay." Bea sounded winded. She clutched her side.

"I CAN'T FIND MY SUNGLASSES. I NEED MY SUNGLASSES. THEY'RE GONE. I CAN'T FIND THEM ANYWHERE!"

"Oh, Cass!" Bea looked alarmed. "You're so distressed! Let me help you look."

Bea searched the desk; Cass searched the dresser. Neither had any success. They decided to split the closet. "You take pants pockets; I'll take shirt pockets," Bea told her. Bea was halfway through the shirts when the phone rang. "I'll let that go," she said, but then whoever it was called back. "Oh, for Pete's sake!" said Bea when she could no longer stand the ringing.

She came right back, but then the doorbell clanged. "Oh, I'm afraid I'm of no use at all," Bea said with a sigh when the timer on the oven buzzed. "This is a terrible day for disasters. You know Doris's Institute opening is tonight?" Cass had forgotten. The oven timer buzzed again. "If I have a second, I'll come back to help," Bea said on her way out.

"Yeah, right," Cass grumbled.

Bea'd heard her. "What did you say?"

"Nothing," said Cass between gritted teeth.

"You said something."

"Oh, you don't care. You *hate* horror movies. They're crass, remember?"

"Oh, Cass," said Bea, looking dismayed. The oven timer buzzed again.

Once Bea was gone, Cass's search got frenzied. She flung the cushions off the armchair. She swept her palm along the top of the mantel, accidentally knocking a framed photo of Sylvia Hempel to the floor. She slithered crocodile-style along the floor and peeked under the furniture. She removed the drawers from her dresser and dumped the contents out. Now every item of clothing Cass owned was in a giant heap.

She decided that maybe the sunglasses had fallen behind her bed, but the bed frame was too heavy to move. She managed to push the mattress halfway off, only she pushed a little too hard, and it slid to the floor, with her on top of it. Cass's bed was an antique four-poster — that meant it was very high. By the time Cass hit the floor — she'd slid headfirst — she was tangled in her quilt and sheets, her legs scissor-kicking the air. The blood was rushing to her face when she heard the familiar voice: "Nice setup."

Cass should have figured Rod Punkin would do something crazy, like show up two hours early. He surveyed the mess admiringly, then cleared a space for himself by the window so he could fiddle with the video camera Doris had lent them.

Annabella stood on the front step, looking confused. "This is where you live?"

By most standards, living in a town house was considered luxurious: In a city as cramped as New York, having the entire floor of a building, let alone three whole floors, was lavish beyond imagination. For Annabella, who lived in a full-service apartment building on Park Avenue, living in a town house was the equivalent of roughing it. "I've never been to a house without a doorman before," she remarked.

While Annabella applied her makeup in the downstairs powder room, Rod loaded a videotape into Doris's video camera, and Cass divided the props according to location. When Lillian arrived, they did the same with the costumes. "Now, we have to return these exactly how we got them," Lillian couldn't help saying one last time.

Considering how very out of control Rod Punkin could be, where the film shoot was concerned, he was shockingly organized. Not to mention polite! On behalf of the crew, he graciously declined Bea's invitation to lunch. "Sorry, we've only got our principal cast member" — he pointed to Annabella — "until the early evening. And our locations" — he meant the streets near Cass's house — "are going to get pretty crowded, seeing as it's a holiday and all."

They were halfway down Sixty-third Street when Cass heard her name being called. She turned back to see Bea standing in front of the house waving something in the air. "One sec," she told the Twists.

"You left these on the breakfast table," Bea said, handing Cass her sunglasses. For the second time this morning, Bea was breathless because of her. "Now, Cass, my darling, have a spectacular shoot."

The first location was the Tramway Diner, which was just east of Cass's house and a block up from the Queensboro Bridge. They had some audio trouble on account of the traffic and the Roosevelt Island cable cars, and the squalling toddler didn't help matters. The waiters were generous about filling Annabella's bowl with oatmeal over and over again — and they didn't get offended when Rod mixed mustard into it. "It has to look more like gruel," he explained.

The second location was Carl Schurz Park. They had a problem with the fake blood for the hatchet scene. Cass kept having to run to the burger place on First Avenue for extra ketchup packets.

They filmed Annabella screaming "More!" at the top of her lungs in several different locations — on the corner of Third Avenue and Sixtieth Street; in front of the line of tourists waiting to get into Serendipity; in the tiny dressing room of the Betsey Johnson store — though it wasn't easy to pull Annabella away from the rack of striped minidresses.

Rod suggested they all give screaming a shot.

"MORE!" screamed Lillian on York Avenue.

"Louder!" Rod instructed.

"MORE!" screamed Lillian on Seventieth Street.

"I think I just saw your tonsils!" he told her.

Cass filmed Rod screaming in front of Orwasher's Bakery. "MOORRRRRRRE!" he bellowed.

The closer to the East River they got, the gustier the wind blew. Rod wanted to do Cass's screaming shot with the water in the background, and he led them to a cul-de-sac overlooking the FDR Drive.

"Wait!" Lillian said as Rod screamed, "ACTION." "No one will believe she's acting if she's wearing those!" She was pointing to Cass's sunglasses. Rod rolled his eyes for only Cass to see, but then said he had to admit, he saw Lillian's point.

Cass removed her glasses and squinted into the East River's glare. Her jacket didn't have pockets, so she placed them on the sidewalk next to her foot.

"Okay," said Rod. "And . . . action!"

Cass opened her mouth to scream. It came out more like a yap.

"You can do better than that!" Rod told her. "Think of something that bugs you."

Cass thought about how she, Penelope, and Tillie were supposed to take Penelope's little brother trick-or-treating tonight.

"More!" she yelped.

"Louder!" Rod bellowed.

Cass thought about her dream about the statues — she'd had it again last night. She thought about Sylvia Hempel, who still wasn't sleeping in her room.

"More!" she yelled.

"That's not the behavior problem I know!" Rod chastised her.

Cass thought about how she had to go to Timberwood in April, which was the cruelest month. She thought about how Doris told Bea, "Maybe this will be a good release." Who were they to say she needed a good release?

A gust of wind smacked her cheek. Out of the corner of her eye, she saw Annabella Blumberg check her watch.

"MOOORRE!"

"Again!" Rod shrieked delightedly.

She thought about what Oliver Twist could have done if he hadn't been so polite. She thought about all those books about orphans who were good and generous and who sometimes even found their parents in the end. She thought about how she'd never find hers.

"MOOOOOOOORRRRRRRRRE!"

She screamed so loud, the doorman from the building across the way called the police. "We have to get out of here now!" warned Rod, explaining that if you were caught filming without a permit in New York City, you could get fined.

"I think I hear a siren!" cried Lillian, and then the Twists were tearing down East End Avenue without looking back. If they had, they might have noticed Cass's sunglasses lying on the sidewalk.

The last shot of the day involved Annabella chasing Lillian across Seventy-second Street. It was evening now, the sun was almost down, and the sky was a bruised purple. Children dressed like Cabbage Patch Kids and New York Yankees marched in U's from one apartment building to the next.

Rod filmed three takes, cutting once because of an errant poodle and again because of an errant trick-or-treater. Then Annabella said she had to go home. She was going to an Elston freshman's Halloween party and needed to get ready. In a desperate ploy to get invited along, Lillian offered to pay for the cab to Annabella's house, claiming she'd get her mom to come pick her up from there. She didn't give Annabella a chance to say no, hailing a cab and pulling her inside.

They sped off, leaving Rod and Cass to lug the equipment, props, and costumes back to Cass's house.

Chapter Eleven

Like most in the area, the town house Cass lived in was both very narrow and very deep. So that from the street it looked as if there could be no more than two rooms per floor, except once you got inside, you kept going back and back, as if the rooms might never stop.

Cass unlocked the front door to hear gabbing voices and blaring music. The foyer smelled like melted butter and baked parmesan cheese. Cass and Rod entered the double-parlor room — New York speak for side-by-side living rooms — to find vases overflowing with chrysanthemums and snack bowls teeming with salted red pistachios. Bea's cheese pennies were stacked beside oozy wheels of yellow Camembert.

Guests spilled from every room. Cass recognized some. There were artists whom Bea represented, artists who were just friends, psychiatrists from the Institute, regular friends. Cass hadn't realized Bea was throwing a pre-party for Doris's opening.

"Well, if it isn't our little Fellinis!" cried Bea when she saw them. She was wearing a chartreuse silk pajama ensemble. There were giant red beads around her neck. "Are you two famished or what?"

Cass hadn't invited Rod to stay for the party — or to come with her to Doris's Institute opening afterward, but she didn't ask him not to stay, either. They stowed the equipment behind the sofa in the study and went out to the sculpture garden, where they settled into metal folding chairs with plates of minis on their laps.

As an art collector, Bea often gave cocktail parties, and minis were her favorite thing to serve. Cass traded Rod two mini hot dogs for a mini cheeseburger, and she exchanged her mini pepperoni pizza for his green pepper one. Neither ate their mini quiche.

Cass recognized one of the bartenders as a photographer Bea sometimes advised — if you worked for Bea, you were usually a struggling artist of some sort. A violinist set up shop in between two statues, and soon Sylvia Hempel appeared. She was surprisingly calm and didn't even beg for minis, and instead settled at Cass's feet to listen to the music. Cass reached down to rub the velvety back of the dog's ear.

What a funny feeling it was to have so much to say, but no need to talk! Maybe it was because her throat still hurt from screaming, or maybe it was the novelty of seeing Rod actually be quiet. Or maybe it was just that they were tired from their long day. Cass could feel it in the flat parts of her feet — *all that running!* — and across her right shoulder blade, where the camera bag had hung. They sipped ginger ale and listened to the music, not saying a word.

At 8:00 P.M., Bea rang a brass cowbell. The Doris Blume Institute for Psychoanalytic Training and Treatment was only four blocks away, and while they were welcome to stick around, it was high time they got the journey under way. The phone rang as partygoers were filing out the door.

"Cass!" one of the caterers yelled. "There's a Tillie on the phone for you!"

"Hello?"

"Hey, what's going on? You were supposed to be here an hour ago. Nathaniel's ready to go trick-or-treating. You will not believe his costume! He's dressed like a dodgeball. Seriously, I don't think the kid's going to fit in the elevator!"

Cass had forgotten her Halloween plans. Out of the corner of her eye, she saw Rod leaning against the wall, waiting for her. He was deep in conversation with the violinist from the party, who he'd just learned had played background on a Rolling Stones album.

"I forgot I had to go to Doris's opening," Cass told the phone. "I know, doesn't this suck? Obviously, I'd rather be with you guys instead of a bunch of adults."

☮ ☮ ☮

The Doris Blume Institute for Psychoanalytic Training and Treatment was a slender white building sandwiched between a pizza parlor and a bakery. Passing through the heavy wooden doors, Cass thought this location couldn't be good for Doris's diet. She heard lots of guests murmuring the same thing.

They entered a room with wood-paneled walls and soft golden light. There were Oriental carpets on the floor, and soft leather chairs in quiet shades of burgundy. Inside, the mood was less giddy than it had been at Bea's house, but no less celebratory. White-haired men with rumpled shirts clinked glasses with curly-haired women in long dresses. In the center of the room, a woman played the harp. Cass and Rod headed straight for the dessert table, where they helped themselves to the pyramid of bite-size éclairs from the bakery next door.

They settled in a quiet spot in the shadow of the spiral staircase and sat on the floor with their backs against the wall. Cass folded her knees underneath her so she didn't trip the people walking by. It was an awkward way to sit, and she had to hunch forward to bite into an éclair.

"So, you're tall, huh?"

Rod's remark had the instant effect of making

Cass feel taller — and not in a good way. Also, she was pretty sure there was chocolate in her teeth.

"I'm five-eight." Cass placed her tongue on the front of her two front teeth, then the back, tasting for chocolate.

"That's tall," said Rod. "My older sister's tall. My parents are always telling her not to slump. My dad calls her turtleback. Nice, huh?"

"Really nice." Cass had a strange and unexpected thought. *My dad didn't know me when I was tall.*

Had Rod been able to read it? "So how did they die?" he asked her.

No one ever asked Cass that.

"In a car accident."

"Were you in the car?"

No one ever asked that, either.

"Nope, though sometimes I think about what if I had been."

She'd never told anyone that.

"I bet," said Rod.

He did?

"They were on vacation. In Europe. It was their second honeymoon. I was mad they were going." The chocolate taste in Cass's mouth turned sour, and she stopped talking out loud. *I was with Doris. We took them to the airport in her blue car. There was a rip in the backseat. My dad let me sit in his lap. I was so short then. He got me a*

snow globe of the city at the airport store. The Statue of
Liberty looked like she had dirt on her face. . . .

Ack! Cass didn't want to be thinking all this! Why
was she thinking all this? They needed to talk about
something else. They needed to talk about Rod! Cass
turned to him. There was a crumb on his bottom lip.
She didn't tell him. "You know how in class, you just
say stuff out of nowhere. Why do you do it?"

"Bored, I guess," replied Rod with a shrug. "And
because it's kind of a rush, too. Seeing how people
react and stuff. My parents are always asking me if I'm
doing it on purpose." He bent his chin toward his
chest and made his voice sound like a deep dad's voice:
"Rod, are you trying to get kicked out of school? Are
you behaving like a lunatic on purpose? Is this your
idea of fun? Making our lives a living hell?"

Rod's imitation made Cass laugh, and then it made
her want Rod not to have to talk about himself anymore. "It's funny, no one ever asks me how my parents
died," she said.

"Not your best friends?"

"I guess they think it's sensitive."

"So what?" said Rod. The crumb was still on his
lip. "It's the most important thing in your life."

Cass didn't like the way this sounded. "No, it's
not," she said. *Is it?* And then more memories entered
her head: *My bangs were in my eyes. My mom said when she*

73

got back, she'd give me a haircut. I couldn't stop crying. I kept saying, "Don't go." I got snot on my sleeve. I felt like a big baby. I got carsick on the way home because Doris didn't have any sucking candy. My mom always had sucking candy.

"Sometimes I wish my parents were dead." Rod's lip curled when he said this, and the crumb fell off.

"Don't go!" she heard the little version of herself wailing. *"Don't go!" Could I have known?* she wondered. *Somewhere, somehow, could I have known?*

At some point during their conversation, the violinist from Bea's party had joined the harp player, and the music had gone from gentle-in-the-background music to something strange and electric-sounding. People weren't dancing, but they'd stopped talking to watch. The harpist plucked so ferociously at the strings, Cass thought her fingers might bleed.

The upturn in the music was actually a signal for people to pay attention. Doris was a woman who tended to toddle, but tonight — dressed in a glittery satin sheath the color of Windex (with matching eye makeup, of course!) — she glided onto the makeshift stage as if she were Annabella Blumberg. She took her place behind the podium. Guests crisscrossed the room to join the semicircle of listeners forming around her.

Doris tapped the microphone. The room erupted in "*Shhhhhhhhh*'s." And then, just when it was finally quiet and Doris's lips were poised to utter the word "Welcome," came Rod's piercing voice. "WE GOTTA GET OUT OF HERE!"

Every head turned to look — only now Cass was sitting by herself, and Rod Punkin was gone.

Chapter Twelve

In seconds, Bea was there.

Her arrival had the effect of a curtain going down in front of Cass's face, shielding her from the eyes in the room. She caught a glimpse of Doris flailing her arms in mad S.O.S. motions to both distill the commotion and take the unwelcome spotlight off Cass. "WELCOME, EVERYONE!" she shouted. Cass detected a tinge of worry in her voice. "WELCOME, WELCOME!"

Bea knelt down to face Cass. "What happened?" she whispered. On Bea's right cheek, there was a smudge of blush that hadn't been rubbed in enough. Cass wanted to touch it.

The Statue of Liberty looked like she had dirt on her face.

Cass's words came out in a frazzled sputter. "I don't know. . . . He was here, then he wasn't. . . . He does that, the blurting. . . . He's got problems."

"Oh, dear," whispered Bea in a way that wasn't at all judgmental but instead was sympathetic. Cass grimaced, surprised at how protective this made her feel. *He doesn't need you to feel sorry for him!* she thought.

Bea interpreted the look on Cass's face as concern. "Don't worry, darling. I don't think he went very far.

We'd have heard if he left the building. I imagine he's around somewhere. . . ." She looked toward the spiral staircase, which was the nearest departure route Rod could have taken. "These speeches won't take very long, and then we'll go look for him, okay?"

I felt like a big baby.

I feel like a big baby.

Cass nodded okay.

"Okay," said Bea. Cass could hear Bea's knees creak as she rose to stand. "Come with me to the front. Doris needs us to man —" Bea chuckled before correcting herself. "I mean woman — *ha!* — the slide projector." Cass said she'd rather stay where she was. Bea seemed to understand. Cass watched her bustle through the crowd toward the front of the room.

Doris was a lively speaker, but Cass felt buzzy and restless the whole time she talked. Nothing could go fast enough. "I'm so thrilled," Doris told the crowd; Cass heard it as a slow-motion drone: *"I'mmmmmmm-mmmmmmmm soooooooooo thriiiiiiilled."* Cass realized she couldn't wait anymore. She stood up quietly. Then, during a moment of loud laughter, she tiptoed quickly toward the spiral staircase, feeling not at all guilty as she began her ascent and Doris's voice grew fainter.

Her day was ending the exact same way it had started. *I'm always looking for something,* she thought. *I'm always losing something, and I'm always looking for something.* Now she was looking for someone. What had happened to Rod? She reached the landing and faced a hallway. It was dark and unfamiliar, and Cass had to hold her arms Frankenstein-style in front of her chest to make sure she didn't bump into anything. It reminded her of when she was little, how she used to shut her eyes and walk around, pretending to be blind. *How could I ever have played such a stupid game?* she wondered.

She tripped on a vacuum cleaner someone had left out, and then she almost screamed. *I could sue!* she thought. *You can't just leave things lying around!* And then she remembered the person she'd be suing would be her aunt, and she wasn't supposed to be up here, any-way. "Rod . . . ," she whispered. "Rod?" Downstairs, she heard Doris pass the microphone to a psychiatrist with a wet-sounding cough. "Rod? Rod? Are you here, Rod?" she whispered.

"*Blurrrrch!*" she heard from downstairs. *Yuck*, she thought. *That guy should see a doctor.* She remembered that psychiatrists were doctors. She fixed her thought. *That guy should see a* real *doctor.*

Her eyes had adjusted to the dark, and now she could see the tiny brass dots along the wall. They were doorknobs. She went from one to the next, turning knobs. Closed. Locked. Jiggled a bit, but still locked. She turned a corner and stumbled over a magazine stand that was next to an armchair and in front of a door. The knob felt cold on her palm. She twisted it left — it opened. A desk lamp lit up the room. It took Cass's eyes a few moments to adjust.

The first things she saw were Rod's black boots. They were resting on the cylindrical headrest of a long leather sofa. Rod was stretched sideways and backward across it. He was holding something silver that he kept inspecting, even when he heard Cass enter.

"How old do you think you are here?" he asked her. "I'm guessing seven or eight. Your hair is all messy. You look like a Beatle, only more punk rock. That's a compliment." He turned the frame toward her so she could see. The little version of herself stared back. *My bangs were in my eyes.* Cass realized this was Doris's office they were in.

She would have thought this would make her more relaxed, but instead she felt tense. Rod's hands were fidgety. The silver frame moved up and down as he held it, making twitchy squares of light on the wall. Alone in the room with this boy who *had* probably been in a mental hospital — or if he hadn't yet, maybe he should have been! — Cass felt both like nothing could go fast enough, but also that all she'd like to do was stand still.

"I saw someone I knew," Rod said, by way of explanation.

If he was hinting at something, Cass didn't get it. "Here? At my aunt's party? But everyone's so old!"

"Well, yeah, he's old," Rod turned to lie on his back. He rested the silver picture frame facedown on his chest and stared up at the ceiling. "They usually are."

They usually are? It wasn't like Cass to be so easily stumped.

"I went to him for almost three years, and then my parents said we had to stop. My dad thought he was filling my head with garbage, that's how he put it. Also, he said that I manipulated the guy. That *I* manipulated the *shrink*!" Rod breathed sharp, furious breaths, and Cass watched the picture of herself go up and down on his chest.

Her legs ached. She crossed the room and took a seat at Doris's desk. She couldn't see Rod's face from this angle. He was taking a break from talking, anyway. Cass opened the top desk drawer and peeked inside. There were pens, a tub of purple lip gloss, some paper clips, a scrap of paper on which Doris had scrawled:

muffin (blueberry) — 550 cal, pizza
(minus the cheese) — 250, cookie
(c. chip) — 250, bad! bad! bad!

There was a picture of Sylvia Hempel, an expired ID card for the Jack LaLanne Fitness Club, and a random key attached to a string.

"I gotta figure, you know from shrinks . . . seeing as your aunt's who she is," continued Rod. "And because of what happened to you. How often do you see yours?"

No one ever asked Cass about this, either.

"I don't," she answered. She touched her finger to the key and dragged it toward her. "I mean, I did, but I don't anymore. I saw her for two years after they died. They're going to make me see someone else." Cass recalled how Doris had said she'd made an appointment for her with "a brilliant specialist in adolescent issues."

Cass pulled the key out of the drawer. The string was thin like dental floss but silky and blue with a little white tag tied to the end. Written on it in slanty letters that were also familiar to Cass were the words M. H. — Front Door.

The sound of feet thumping down the hallway caught Cass off guard, and she slammed the drawer shut. It made a giant bang, rattling the desk and the lamp on top of it. It blinked off and on, like the scene in a horror movie right before you're supposed to scream.

The thumping feet were getting closer. There were voices. Cass was pretty sure she heard a *blurrrrch* sound. Rod was sitting up now. His face was darting eyeballs and twitching lips. He tugged at his earlobe. Cass was ready for him to do it. *Here it comes,* she thought to herself. But, this time, Rod whispered instead of screamed, "Take cover!" And then he tumbled onto the floor and rolled under the sofa, somehow managing to take the silver picture frame with him. The voices were on the other side of the door.

Cass fell to her knees, then scooted under the desk. She heard the doorknob jiggle, then felt something tickle her face. It was the string attached to the key, which was hanging off the desk. Cass pulled it down toward her, then jammed it into the pocket of her jeans, reminding herself to return it to its proper place when this was over.

The door opened, and Cass wondered what would happen when Doris saw them. Rod couldn't keep quiet. He'd proven that. They wouldn't get in trouble — Cass had never once gotten in trouble. But she might feel kind of dumb. "I know it's in here," she heard her aunt Doris say. "In a folder . . ." Cass heard the sound of heavy footsteps pivot. "A blue folder . . . should say 'Caterer' on it. Ah, yes, there it is —"

"Blurrrrch," replied her companion. Doris was with the guy with the bad cough.

Cass hugged her knees tightly to her chest, mashing her nose into the space between. It had been such a long day, and she'd done so many things and been so many places, she couldn't figure out what her jeans smelled like — if they smelled like anything. Was that a trace of fake-blood ketchup? Was that oatmeal? Was that Sylvia Hempel, who on a hot day smelled like toast and on a rainy day smelled like a wet sweater? Today it had been nothing out — only windy. What did Sylvia Hempel smell like on a windy day? How could Cass not know?

Cass could feel Doris bending over the desk. The sound of Doris's hands sweeping along the top of the desk sounded thunderous from underneath. "Okay, got it!" Doris said with a hefty clap. "Next on the agenda — finding my niece! You didn't see her, did you?"

The man coughed something indiscernible, though Cass figured — considering he didn't even know her — he'd said no.

"Interesting," Doris half-sang. "Ooooh!" Her voice rose a notch, like she'd just seen a mouse. Cass's stomach clutched. *This is it,* she thought.

Doris kept talking. "I forgot to say — did you see she had a date with her? Isn't that the most adorable thing? She's not even thirteen! She's hot stuff, my Cass!"

Hot stuff! Just hearing the dumb phrase made Cass's cheeks burn. It didn't matter if they never left, Cass was never coming out, anyway. Finally, the door clicked shut. The thumps on the carpet got farther away.

Cass listened for signs of Rod. Could he have gotten out? Was she alone? "Are you there?" she called, staying put.

Rod wasn't eager to move, either. His voice sounded muffled and distant, coming from under the sofa. "That was him," he said.

"Who was him?" Cass asked.

"The guy with your aunt Doris. My head tripper, my shrink. The guy I didn't want to see."

"The guy with the cough?" Rod spent all that time with the guy with the gunky throat?

"Yeah. . . ."

"Wow."

"He's got a sinus condition." Rod sounded almost wistful when he said this.

Cass leaned her head against the inside wall of the desk. She heard rustling sounds, and Rod's voice getting closer. He'd come out from under the sofa, then taken a seat on the other side of the desk.

Were it not for the thick slab of mahogany between them, their heads would have been touching.

CASS'S PERSONAL FAVORITE WORDS

carbuncular

conniption

punchy

kicky

slaphappy

chaotic

idiotic

hypochondriac

idiosyncratic

cantankerous

hoi polloi

riffraff

zigzag

shim sham

preposterous

stalwart

fussbudget

Chapter Thirteen

The next day, Cass went over to Penelope's house to watch rented movies on the Schwartzbaums' brand-new videocassette recorder. Penelope and Tillie preferred romantic comedies to horror movies, so Cass was bored for most of the time.

She helped Penelope's brother, Nathaniel, organize his Halloween candy. First, they did it by color, but then decided to do it by category — chocolate, fruity, lollipop, gum, and miscellaneous for the Mary Janes and Bit-O-Honeys. Nathaniel hated nuts, and so he let Cass have the miniature Mr. Goodbars and Snickers. And he gave her a handful of Peanut Chews.

I love you more than Peanut Chews.

I love you more than kangaroos.

Nathaniel liked to ask questions. "Where are your sunglasses?"

Cass looked in her jacket pocket so she could show them to him, but they weren't there. "I must have left them at home," she said, feeling the panic of yesterday morning returning. She tried to ignore it.

"How's Sylvia Hempel?"

"Fine."

"How come you didn't bring her?"

" 'Cause your mom doesn't let dogs into the house."

"How come?"

"I don't know. She's your mom."

"Yeah. Why are Swedish Fish called Swedish Fish, do you think?"

"I have no idea."

"Want to play Geography? I'll go first. Albuquerque. That ends with an E not a Y, in case you didn't know."

"Ethiopia."

"Afghanistan."

Penelope and Tillie kept shushing them. "We're just at the good part!" they kept saying. Every time they said this, Cass would look at the screen and see people kissing. How come the good part was always people kissing?

"New York."

"Kansas."

"Siberia."

"How come so many countries end in A?"

"So how was the filming?" Penelope asked once the movie was over. "And what'd you do after?"

"I told you," Cass said. "I mean, I told Tillie." *Hadn't Tillie told Penelope?* "I had to go to Doris's opening."

"That's it?" Penelope asked.

"What else would there be?"

87

Tillie shrugged. "You tell us."

"So how was trick-or-treating?" Cass asked, turning the tables.

"There was a party in the building. We ran into Annabella and Lillian."

"Oh, yeah?" said Cass.

"Mmmm-hmmmmm," said Penelope and Tillie at once.

Cass and Tillie both lived on the Upper East Side, but that evening, Tillie had to go to tap-dancing class with her mother. So Cass walked her to the dance studio on the way to the bus stop.

It was the first day of November, and the store windows on Broadway were cluttered with the trappings of Thanksgiving. Morris Brothers sold rugby shirts in autumnal stripes, like orange and brown or yellow and green. Chocolate turkeys formed a procession in the window of the Broadway Nut Shop.

"You know why I have to take tap? Because my mom wants me to have all the opportunities she didn't have," Tillie said.

Cass had heard about this before. "Oh, yeah?" she said, trying to sound like she hadn't.

"She says what happened to her *is not* going to happen to me."

"What happened to her?"

"She lost herself over a guy is what she says happened. Meaning my dad, obviously. She says she wasted half her life, and now she's making up for lost time."

Cass had heard that if you didn't get a good night's sleep, it was impossible to make it up the next night. If you couldn't make up for lost sleep, could you make up for lost time?

"So, guess what she wants to do! She wants to go on a safari. In Africa! A real safari, not like the kind at Great Adventure. Anyway, she thinks I should go with her. I told her I have school, but she says it's educational; they'll understand. I think she's forgotten what type of place Elston Prep is. Plus, and this is scary, she talks about moving all the time."

"Where?" Cass hadn't heard *this* before. "Are you going to move downtown? That'd be so weird if you lived downtown!"

"No, not moving in the city. Moving *out* of the city. Like to a different state — and not New Jersey." Cass really hadn't heard *this* before.

"She picks a different place every week practically. Now she thinks we should move to Santa Fe. I don't even know where Santa Fe is! Is it in Texas or California?"

Cass told her she thought it was in New Mexico.

"I don't want to move. But I can't stay here with my dad, obviously."

"You're not going to have to move," Cass said, trying to sound consoling. "Don't worry."

"I sure hope so," Tillie said.

But if you did move . . . Cass had the beginning of a thought that led to the kind she knew she needed to keep to herself. "Don't worry," she told Tillie again. "You're not moving."

They walked quietly for a block.

"Oh," said Tillie as they waited for the light to cross the street. "I forgot to tell you. I decided on peace."

Cass looked confused. Tillie's voice sounded surprised that she had to remind her. "You know, for my bat mitzvah. As the theme. Don't worry, I'm going to make a care package for you. Everyone's getting peace buttons and peace T-shirts. And my mom says we can even save you a slice of cake — it's going to be chocolate with yellow frosting and a humongous rainbow-colored peace sign." The light turned green. "You know the one good thing about the fact that you're going to Timberwood then?"

Cass said she didn't.

"I can invite Lillian Lang, but I know she can't

come. Of course, I'd take a million Lillian Langs if you *could* come. I'm just saying, it's a good consolation."

Cass wasn't sure how to respond. She didn't have to, because Tillie kept going. "Speaking of Lillian," she said, giving Cass a look that said *I have something important to say.* "When we saw her last night, she said you and Rod Punkin were really close. She says he was probably at your house. We told her it wasn't true, because if it was, we'd know. But, Cass, I don't really believe that. I feel like you're leaving me out. Penelope does, too."

Did Tillie know how crazy that sounded? *Penelope and I feel this way. You're leaving us out! Two of us! One of you!*

Sometimes, Cass thought, *when people get mad at you for not telling them stuff — it makes you not want to tell them stuff.*

"Yoooo-hooooooo! Girls!"

Cherry Warner was waiting on the corner of Eightieth and Broadway, already dressed for tap-dancing class. She wore a shiny black leotard with a matching skirt that cut diagonally up her thigh, magenta tights, and high-heeled silver shoes. Like Tillie, she had hair an almost neon shade of orange.

"Don't mind me if I'm distracted. I'm trying to remember the routine. Tell me if I'm wrong, Till, is it double-hop-step-dig-slap-hop-double-hop-step-dig-slap-hop?" Cherry asked Tillie.

"Mom!"

"What?"

"You're dancing in the middle of the street!"

Cherry Warner tipped up her head to the street sign, as if she had to make sure that was correct. "Well, I always wanted to dance on Broadway." She giggled. Tillie flashed Cass a mortified look. "Get it?" Cherry Warner chirped. "Broadway? A Broadway dancer? Dance on Broadway? So, do I have the routine right?"

"Yeah, but you scuff instead of slap, and the second hop is a tog," Tillie mumbled, embarrassed. Cass knew she was supposed to feel bad for her friend, but what she was really thinking was that she'd never realized tap dancing had so many good words. They'd make a good word list.

"Good-bye, toots!" Cherry Warner cried with a shuffle tog. Tillie half-waved, then she and her mother went inside.

"Bye," Cass said.

Because his dad had access to professional video-editing facilities, it was Rod Punkin's responsibility to cut *Olivia Twisted* together. He did so in two late-night sessions from which he telephoned Cass repeatedly. Sometimes, he wanted her opinion on the music he'd chosen for certain scenes. Sometimes, he just wanted to tell her something. "Wait till you see the title sequence. It looks so rad! You're gonna die!" Or "Your name looks so great on-screen. Don't tell anyone, but I left it up for five seconds longer than Lillian and Annabella's. Not that they'll notice . . ."

On the Friday the Twists were supposed to make their presentation, Ms. Glitch was home sick with a cold. So, Rod had extra time to work on stuff. "I hope you don't mind, but I amped up the shot of you screaming," he called to say. "In this one shot, you look just like that picture of you as a little kid with your hair all messed up. You look like hot stuff!" Cass hung up on him after that, but she was laughing as she did.

Rod was still one of the eighth grade's favorite topics. First-semester progress reports had gone out, and the rumor was that Rod Punkin had gotten seven marks for bad behavior — this was an enormous triumph, considering eighth graders took only six classes. The gym teacher, it turned out, had sent two.

That next Friday morning, Cass woke up feeling like a little kid who was dumb enough to feel excited to go to school. "Today is the day is the day is the day!" she yelled, swooping seagull-like upon the breakfast table. "Gotta go," she shouted between bites of toasted rye, sending a fountain of crumbs into the air. *"Adios! Arrivederci! Sayonara! Ciao!"*

Bea told her to hold on one sec, a package had arrived for her. "Someone put it through the slot this morning," Bea said. Cass was shocked to see a brown envelope with her name on it.

Inside was the videotape for *Olivia Twisted*, and a note from Rod that said:

I WON'T FORGET YOU.

Chapter Fourteen

"He was expelled!"

"Did you hear? Rod Punkin was expelled!"

"Who's Rod Punkin?"

"The crazy kid who talked during class."

"Oh, him? Wow. I thought he was funny."

"Yeah, funny as in funny farm."

"Well, I heard he's a genius — he has a 300 IQ."

"You can't have a 300 IQ!"

For nearly a week, Rod Punkin's expulsion from Elston was the eighth grade's favorite topic. But then midterms were announced, and talk turned to what percentages exams would count for, how unfair that was, and how it sucked because eighth-grade marks *really* counted for college. Quickly, everyone forgot about Rod. It was like he'd been expelled twice — first from school, then from people's memories.

This wasn't the case for Cass, of course. On the day Rod was expelled, the Twists presented *Olivia Twisted* for which they received a standing ovation — the claps sounded flat and fleshy to Cass: In one ear, she heard Lillian Lang yelling, *"They love us!"* but in the other, she heard a voice, maybe hers, asking, *"What happened to Rod?"* That afternoon, Cass opted out of a trip to Sam Goody to buy records with Penelope and Tillie, instead rushing home to call him. As the day wore on, the voice in her head had gotten more demanding. *WHAT HAPPENED TO ROD?*

A man answered the phone at Rod's house. He sounded like he had pebbles in his mouth. "Rod's not here. But I can try and get a message to him." The man told Cass to hold on, he'd get a pen, but then she was pretty sure he didn't get one, and that when she rattled off the digits to her number, she was saying them to air. She replayed his words in her head several times: *"I can try"* not *"I will." "I can try and get it to him"* not *"I'll give it to him."* As if getting it to him required more than simply telling him or slipping a piece of paper under his bedroom door.

She called again the next afternoon — this time, she got a little kid on the line. "Hello, is Rod there?" she asked.

"Nope!" the kid barked. It was a boy. "Rod's at boring school!"

"What?" Cass asked, not because she hadn't heard, but because she had no idea what he meant.

The kid acted like Cass was a moron and answered her question as slowly as possible: "I saiiiiiiid, Roooood's aaaaaat borrrrrrrr —"

There was a scuffle in the background and a sharp woman's voice: "Who's that on the phone?"

"Mario from the pizza parlor," Cass heard the boy inexplicably lie.

"Pizza! We're not having pizza! Louisa made pot roast, and you're ordering a pizza! I don't *think* so. . . ."

Cass's eardrum shook when the boy dropped the phone — she kept listening: There were distant sounds of yelling, then a grumbling noise that made Cass wonder if the phone had fallen into the food processor. "Hello!" she shouted, imagining that if a voice could get chopped up, hers was being sliced and diced and pureed. "Hello?!" There was a quick succession of clicks, then static, then the operator stupidly informing her there appeared to be a receiver off the hook.

Cass figured she'd have to wait for Rod to get in touch with her. But a week went by, then another, and he still hadn't called. For Cass, life beyond school became a long jittery exercise in waiting for the phone to ring. It never did. So, Cass placed her hopes on the mailman — Rod was a note writer, after all.

She'd get home from school, then wait agitatedly on the stoop for the mailman to come. Every day, it was art catalogs and bills for Bea and nothing for Cass. Winter had come early this year, and after an hour in the cold, Cass's teeth chattered. Even in her mittens, her hands felt dead and rubbery. Was this what "reckless with misery" meant?

Seeing how despondent Cass was, Bea tried to help, but after calling Rod's parents twice, there was nothing much more she could do. "They were perfectly evasive," she spat in frustration. "That poor fabulous boy!"

To make matters worse, Cass hadn't found her sunglasses — though not for lack of trying. Several times she'd scoured the spot on East End Avenue where she'd thought she'd left them. In her most pitying moments, Cass saw something fitting about losing the sunglasses not once but twice in one day.

No matter how many things in your life you'd already lost — even if your life was a gigantic festering pile of loss! — you could always lose more.

If anyone aside from Cass was clinging to the memory of Rod Punkin, it was Ms. Glitch, who, weeks after Rod's expulsion, was still calling Rod's name during attendance. "Oh, right, yes," mumbled the teacher absentmindedly when she remembered. She shook her head forlornly, then promptly neglected to erase Rod's name from her roll book. Cass thought the teacher's behavior was strange, but she appreciated it.

Rod had left a hole in English class — it was nice to know someone else felt it.

The closest Cass and the teacher came to discussing Rod outright was when Cass mistakenly turned in a grammar assignment with a word list written on the back. It was called: THE MANY WAYS TO SAY YOU'RE EXPELLED, and included boot, banish, chuck, oust, eject, kick out, release, throw out, drive out, exorcise, eliminate, and jettison.

IS THIS A POEM? the red pen at the top of the page wanted to know. IF IT ISN'T, IT COULD BE!

YOU ARE CORDIALLY INVITED
TO A TEX-MEX FIESTA
AT THE HOME OF
CHERRY AND TILLIE WARNER
TO
CELEBRATE

THE BEGINNING OF

WINTER VACATION,

THE END OF 1982,

AND OTHER MISCELLANEOUS,

EXTREMELY IMPORTANT EVENTS. . . .

Chapter Fifteen

If for Bea a home were an expression of who she was, for Cherry Warner a home was who she wanted to be — and for the moment, Cherry Warner wanted to be anything having to do with the color salmon. Everywhere, every place Cass looked there was salmon: a crushed-velvet salmon sofa, a salmon settee, a salmon rug. Even the walls were salmon, covered in a textured silk that looked like a thumbprint from up close.

Cherry Warner was even serving salmon! She greeted the girls wearing an apron with **COWGIRLS DO IT BETTER!** written on it in fire-red rope letters and underlined with a lasso. She barely said hello before rattling off the menu. "Salmon and black bean fajitas, chicken breasts with mole sauce, and for the grand fiesta finale, crispy banana chimichangas topped with *dulce con leche!*"

The girls waited on the salmon sofa while Cherry Warner put the finishing touches on dinner. "She says salmon's the new flounder, whatever that means," Tillie whispered, and rolled her eyes. A song called "La Bamba" played on the stereo.

It turned out Cass and Penelope weren't the only guests attending the fiesta, and when the doorbell rang, Cass was shocked to see Doris and Bea with Sylvia Hempel in tow. They wore giant straw sombreros on their heads and colorful fringed ponchos draped over their shoulders. Even the dog was dressed appropriately Tex-Mex with a bandana tied around her neck. Bea and Doris carried bouquets of wildflowers for Tillie and Cherry and loads of different-colored shopping bags — so many that Bertrand, the elevator man, had to help. Apparently, he was in on whatever was going on, too.

"Surprised?" he asked, looking directly at Cass.

Doris embraced her in a giant bear hug.

"Surprise!" she sang into Cass's ear, and planted a giant kiss on her cheek — somehow she'd had the foresight to wear salmon-colored lip gloss. "What a momentous occasion when our Cass turns thirteen!"

Could Cass's problem with losing things have gotten so bad that she'd lost track of time? Was her birthday today?

For weeks, Bea had been asking her what she wanted to do on "the big day." For weeks, Cass had been thinking: *Soon, I'll finally be thirteen*. Cass gazed down the line of expectant faces, feeling dizzy and discombobulated.

It was winter break, and the days did sometimes blend together. Still, was it really possible that Cass had woken up, eaten breakfast, watched a movie, read a book, and talked on the phone to Penelope, all without realizing "the big day" was today? Cass remembered how Tillie had said Cherry Warner had both lost herself and time.

Has that happened to me?

"We know, we know," said Tillie, misconstruing Cass's addled expression. "Your birthday isn't until tomorrow. But since I have bat mitzvah lessons all afternoon and Penelope has an orthodontist's appointment, we thought we'd celebrate tonight. Mom says fiestas take a long time, so you'll be here when your real birthday officially starts."

Only Bea seemed to notice that Cass was reeling for a more complicated reason than simply being surprised. She asked Cass to come with her to the kitchen to help get Sylvia Hempel some water.

Bea wasn't a person who got easily rattled. "Oh, dear, oh, dear," she muttered nervously while looking for a bowl in Cherry Warner's kitchen cupboards.

"Oh, dear what?" asked Cass.

"You forgot, didn't you?"

"I didn't forget. I mean, I knew my birthday was coming, I just lost track of the days."

"A child shouldn't forget her birthday," Bea's voice wobbled.

"I'm not a child!" blurted Cass, then she remembered that wasn't the point. "I didn't forget!" she added quickly.

But the idea that Cass could have forgotten her own birthday seemed to disturb Bea to the core. She opened up a cupboard without even glancing inside, then clapped it shut. She repeated this several times. "I forgot what I was looking for," she remarked unhappily. Cass handed her a Tupperware bowl from the dish rack.

Cass stared at Bea's hands turning on the kitchen faucet. They looked blue and cordy, and maybe even like they were shaking.

"I'm just surprised, Bea, that's all." Cass tried to sound gentle. "Really."

Bea turned the faucet off and for several long moments stood staring into the empty sink basin. Cass hoped she wouldn't cry.

"Just as long as you're okay with this," Bea said finally, motioning to the dining room — they could hear predinner jabbering. "Cherry did go to a lot of trouble, but this is your birthday," Bea said, as if she needed to remind her again. Cass nodded, feeling strange.

Bea grimaced, then sounded purposely lighthearted. "Seriously, all you need to do is signal me, and

I'll feign stomach flu." Bea clutched her belly, and gave Cass a woozy look. "I tell you, I'm a pro. We'll be out of here in a minute flat." She handed the water bowl to Cass. Some splashed on the floor.

"Chow's on!" screamed Cherry from the dining room. And Cass's thirteenth-birthday fiesta was officially under way.

Gifts were supposed to make you feel like you'd been given something, so how come Penelope and Tillie's first gift made Cass feel the exact opposite?

"Open this one first!" Tillie commanded gleefully, passing Cass a narrow white box with a Pandemonium sticker on the top.

"Pandemonium! I don't know if I like the sound of that." Bea chuckled. Tillie explained that it was a store on Broadway with buttons, colored T-shirts, and lots of new-wave stuff.

Cass dug her finger into the wad of black and purple tissue papers and removed a pair of brand-new heart-shaped sunglasses, red plastic ones with black lenses.

"And these ones aren't missing an eye!" Tillie announced as if this was spectacular news.

"But we could take out the left lens if you want," offered Penelope.

"Thanks," said Cass, missing her old glasses.

They had other gifts, too: a collage made up of magazine ads and funny sayings — Bea pronounced it "masterfully creative"; a mixed tape with songs by the Cars, the Beatles, and Elvis Costello; and woven friendship anklets, like the ones Lillian Lang wore around her wrist. "We each have them." Penelope unrolled her tube sock for everyone to see. "There are three beads in the middle to represent three best friends!"

Doris gave Cass two big boxes and one little one. The first big one was from Betsey Johnson, a name Cass recognized from filming *Olivia Twisted*. Inside was the kind of outfit Doris said she'd have chosen for herself — if she could actually fit into something so teensy. It was a miniskirt with black and red diagonal stripes and two matching tops — one was all black with a band of red along the bottom, the other was red with a black band at the bottom. There was a pair of black tights and a pair of red tights.

Cass held each item up for everyone to see — there were oohs and ahhs. Penelope said that was the very skirt she'd wanted. "The saleswoman said this is all the rage with girls your age," Doris said. She pointed to a second package. "She told me to buy these, too." Cass opened the box — inside were large black boots with big laces and round toes — like the ones Rod wore. "I hate that they're called combat boots," Doris told the crowd. "But I think they look cool."

Bea's gifts were elaborately wrapped in an assortment of patterned papers. Each had its own card — so Cass knew which gifts were from Bea, which ones were from Sylvia Hempel, and which were from both. There was a blue turtleneck sweater (from Bea); fuzzy red gloves (from Sylvia Hempel); and a book about classic horror films (from both). The largest box was from Bea, Sylvia Hempel, and Doris, too — it was a video camera exactly like the one she'd borrowed to shoot *Olivia Twisted*.

She wished she could tell Rod.

The last gift Cass opened was from Bea alone. "I was rooting through some old stuff, when I found this," Bea told her. It was a soft leather book. Engraved in chunky black letters in the bottom right-hand corner were the words: THE COTTAGE AT 2 MARCH HARE ROAD.

Inside the scrapbook were photographs of the cottage, pictures of the farm across the way, a snapshot of her parents sitting cross-legged in the grass, a watercolor someone had painted of Bea sitting on the porch, a picture of Cass. *My bangs were in my eyes.* There was a handmade label from a bottle of the apple cider Cass used to drink.

There was a map of the area. Underneath, someone had written — *Is that my mother's handwriting?* — Life on M. H. Road.

M. H.

March Hare Road. M. H. — FRONT DOOR. That's what the key in Doris's office had on it.

On the last page, there was a dried flower. "That's from the garden in the backyard. It's a grape hyacinth," Bea told everyone. "The Berkshires are known for them."

"The Berkshires? Is that where this cottage was?" Cherry Warner asked.

"Still is," said Bea. "Though we don't go there anymore."

"Well, you two should pay attention," Cherry told Tillie and Penelope, "since you're going there next week!" She meant Timberwood.

"I had no idea that's where Timberwood was," Bea said.

"It will be familiar ground to you, Cass," Cherry Warner remarked.

"Maybe," mumbled Cass, who at that moment was feeling the opposite of familiar. Sitting in this salmon room, celebrating a birthday she'd nearly forgotten, her stomach churning from one too many chimichangas, her fingertip grazing a five-year-old hyacinth from the garden she used to play in, very little felt familiar — except the odd sensation that, at that moment, she was not where she was supposed to be.

Chapter Sixteen

The Upper East Side was one of the quietest neighborhoods in Manhattan, and at this time of night, you could go for blocks without seeing a soul.

Crossing Lexington Avenue, Cass thought about how all through the fiesta, she'd missed Rod and how ridiculous this was. How could she, of all people, be stuck on missing someone? Her! Cass! If there was anything she'd gotten used to in her thirteen years of existence, it was missing people! It was a fact of her life — like having straight hair or being tall. *This is crazy, this is wrong!* And then Cass started to feel something new: She started to feel mad.

First, at Rod: Why hadn't he called? He could have found a way to call! He certainly could have found a way to write!

Then, at Penelope and Tillie: How could they have gotten her those sunglasses when they knew how she felt about her old ones?

At Cherry Warner, for making chimichangas: They'd settled at the bottom of her stomach like lumps of dried-up Play-Doh.

At herself, for taking seconds: She'd been full already — why had she eaten another chimichanga?

At Doris, for buying her clothes: Everyone knew she didn't care about clothes! Though, she had to admit, she liked the boots. . . .

At Sylvia Hempel, for stopping short in the middle of the street to sniff disgusting rotting vegetables outside Gristedes Supermarket. And for *still* sleeping in Bea's room every night.

At Bea, for wearing that stupid sombrero, which kept blowing off her head. "Oh, no!" Bea sobbed as the sombrero lifted itself into the night air. For the millionth time, Cass went tearing after it.

That night, Cass had the dream about the sculptures again. It was the same dream as always, only a gauzy layer of new snow covered the sculptures' faces, obscuring their expressions and making them look even smoother.

She woke with a jolt, shaken and humiliated: Was this the kind of nightmare future horror-movie makers should have? *Nothing happened!* she thought. *Where was the violence? The bloodshed? There wasn't even a hatchet!*

The only way Cass could fall back to sleep was to recite her mother's old poem out loud. "I love you more than cinnamon toast," she told her empty room. "I love you more than the whole East Coast."

Still, in the morning, she had the dream again.

Now there were dusky gray figures flitting among the statues, falling in and out of focus. Cass only glimpsed the figures before they popped out of sight, but she was pretty sure she recognized them. First, she'd seen her parents, then she'd seen Rod.

Cass may have had the dream about the sculptures all night, but she awoke with images of the cottage in her head. In the dusty light of morning, she lay in her bed and put the pieces together.

The cottage is in the Berkshires.

Timberwood is in the Berkshires.

I took a key from Doris's desk drawer with the initials M. H. on it.

M. H. stands for March Hare Road.

And then a thought came to Cass that was more a decision than a thought, because it would stay with her for months to come, and everything she did would be because of it. The thought was: *That's where I'm supposed to be.*

Cass would always look back to the morning of her thirteenth birthday, when she woke up thinking about the cottage and realized: *That's where I'm supposed to be.*

Chapter Seventeen

Cass didn't know what she'd do with the decision yet. She left it sitting in the back of her head, waiting to be acted on.

Second semester started, Penelope and Tillie left for Timberwood, and a storm swooped into New York City. Hacking coughs of thunder shook the window next to Cass's bed, and feverish splats of lightning lit up the bedroom. She awoke to hear footsteps on the stairs, then Bea's voice through the closed door. "Cass, that was school calling. It's a snow day." Cass thought about the many ways she might spend her day, then fell back asleep.

It was a funny thing about sleeping late. The longer you slept, the more sluggish you felt when you finally got up. "Good morning," Cass said drearily, flumping into her seat. An onion roll awaited her. It was 11:00 A.M.

"I love a snow day," said Bea dreamily, glancing up from her coffee cup. "It's like the whole world comes to a stop. Everyone, no matter who, has to put the little problems of life aside." Cass slathered Nutella onto her onion roll and took a bite. Crumbs and chocolate caked the roof of her mouth. Bea switched on the radio.

"This is WYNY, the voice of New York City, and there's only one word to describe today, and that's snow. The Big Apple is covered in it!"

A man from the sanitation department came on to talk about garbage pickups, a woman from the health department told listeners to put salt on their stoops. A representative from the ASPCA warned about the hazards of salt on pets' paws. The traffic reporter said the West Side Highway was slow-moving, the Major Deegan was at a standstill, and Hudson River crossings were backed up for hours.

"Animals, traffic, garbage collection. That's all that matters on a day like today," Bea remarked. "Weather, it's the great equalizer. Today New York City's a small town."

They took cups of tea into the greenhouse, where they stood inside, looking out. The sculptures were mostly covered, except for the occasional hand peeking out of the snow. Cass wondered for a moment if she'd woken up in her dream world, and was relieved to hear the telephone — the telephone never rang in her dreams.

Bea answered it, then returned to say that Penelope's mother was on the phone. She wanted to speak to Cass.

As much as Cass liked Penelope's little brother, Nathaniel, she thought the kid could be a royal pain sometimes. Obviously, she had better things to do on a snow day than babysit a nine-year-old. But it was hard to say no to Denise Schwartzbaum, who was a very persuasive woman, to say the least.

"I'll be eternally grateful to you, Cass," Mrs. Schwartzbaum said in her typically commanding way. "I have a client lunch in an hour, and who knows if I can get a taxi. I've got no help, and with Penelope out in the godforsaken tundra, I'm in a terrible bind. I can't afford to not make this lunch, and I can't afford to bring Nathaniel with me. I'm sure you understand."

Cass was going to say that she was busy, that she had homework, but then she heard Nathaniel in the background. "I'm *nine!*" he was yelling. "I can be by myself!" And the thought that he'd been hearing his mother say she couldn't afford to bring him to some dumb lunch gave Cass a lump in her throat. Mrs. Schwartzbaum offered her five dollars an hour; Cass asked for seven. They settled on six.

Cass went upstairs to change. Her problem with losing things wasn't helped by the fact that ever since tearing her room apart to look for the sunglasses, it had remained a total mess. She could only find one rubber boot, and was about to call

Mrs. Schwartzbaum to cancel, when she spied the pile of birthday gifts, still in boxes in the corner.

The combat boots fit perfectly.

Bea was right. There was something different about New York City today. Usually people walked fast and furious, without looking from side to side. Today they strode, stopping to admire the hills of snow, piled like beach dunes high atop cars. No one wore suits. And people even chatted — strangers in New York City were chatting!

"Some weather!" said the doorman on the corner.

"Don't slip!" an old lady called out.

"I heard by afternoon it'll be coming down in droves," said a man on the bus.

Cass arrived at the Schwartzbaums' apartment building on West End Avenue to find Nathaniel waiting in the lobby under the watch of Carlos, the doorman. *"¡Hola, Señorita Cassandra!"* Carlos insisted on calling Cass, Cassandra — no matter how many times she told him that wasn't her name. "You know who Cassandra was, right?" Cass nodded yes, but as always Carlos told her, anyway. "The truth teller! A mortal woman who can see the future! What do you predict for me, Cassandra?"

"I predict the next time I come here, you'll call me Cassandra. *Even though my name's Cass!"* she said, trying not to laugh.

"Hmmmmmmmm . . ." Carlos gave his chin a thoughtful scratch. "We shall see . . . we shall see." He chuckled. "So, you're here to take this scoundrel off my hands?" He pointed toward the couch, where Nathaniel, in a puff of a down coat and giant moon boots, sat quietly immersed in an Archie Comics Double Digest, behaving nothing like a scoundrel. "Nathaniel, your chariot awaits!"

The boy hopped off the couch. "Hi, Cass! Is my mom really paying you six dollars an hour? Can you lend me five dollars? I want to buy a Duncan Imperial. I have two Butterflies and two Jewels. I can do shoot the moon, walk the dog, rock the cradle, and sometimes I can do sleep — but I'm not very good." It took Cass a few seconds to figure out that Nathaniel was talking about yo-yos.

They got on the Eighty-sixth Street crosstown going east toward Cass's house because Nathaniel said he wanted to see Sylvia Hempel. Buses in New York City were usually slow-moving, but today the crosstown barely inched across Central Park, and when it finally emerged at Fifth Avenue, it sunk to a stop.

"THAT'S IT!" the bus driver shouted. "NEW YORK CITY STREETS ARE OFFICIALLY CLOSED!"

Chapter Eighteen

Cass had never tried to imagine New York City without cars, because she'd never known it could happen. And had she been able to imagine it, she didn't know if she'd have come up with this. Kids were having a snowball fight in the middle of Park Avenue. Little girls lay in the island in the middle of the street, making snow angels. A teenager slid by in a makeshift sled made from the rubber top of a garbage can.

Cass and Nathaniel picked the corner of Lexington and Eighty-fourth Street to build a snowman. They were gathering snow to make the head when Nathaniel screamed, "THAT'S MY FRIEND! THAT'S MY FRIEND!" There was something sad about how he screamed it — like he was just as excited to *have* a friend as he was to run into one. "MATTY! MATTY! YOO-HOO, MATTY! COME HERE!" Cass watched a skinny boy in a silver coat cross toward them. "You'll like him," Nathaniel whispered to her. "He lies all the time."

Cass didn't have a chance to ask what that meant before the spiky-haired boy was standing before them. He was a shifty-eyed kid and a big chatterer who turned out to be an industrious builder. Soon, Cass and Nathaniel's snowman had a snow woman pal, a couple of snow dogs, and even some snow cats. They got hot chocolates from the deli, which they sipped from paper cups while surveying their work.

Nathaniel's friend had a sharp-sounding voice. "My brother has those," he said, pointing to Cass's feet. "He wears them every day, even in summer. They make his feet stink so bad, my mom took them and threw them out in the trash. We had to rescue them from the Dumpster. She's not my brother's mom, she's his stepmom. He hates her, and I don't blame him."

"Oh, yeah?" said Cass, half-listening because she figured these were lies.

"Uh-huh," said the boy. "But she can't take his boots from him now. Nope, she can't. Know why? He's gone." Nathaniel asked what he meant by "gone." "I mean, gone, you dope! Don't you know the word 'gone.' G-O-N-E. Gone. Sent away. I'm not supposed to know, but I know where he is." The kid turned his spiky head from one side to the next, to see if anyone nearby could hear him. "Don't tell anyone, but my brother's at boring school!"

At which point, a harsh lady's voice came hurtling across the street. "MATTY PUNKIN, YOU ARE IN SO MUCH TROUBLE!"

Life in the city may have come to a standstill, but Cass's brain had never worked so quickly. She took it upon herself to apologize to the woman, who wasn't very friendly, but still had the gall to ask if Cass would watch her son for a second longer, because she needed to get to the dry cleaner's to pick up her husband's suit. Did Cass think the dry cleaner's was open?

Cass thought it definitely wasn't. Just about every store on the Upper East Side was closing, if not already closed. And who needed a suit during a blizzard? But she swiftly lied and said, "Sure, probably. I think I saw that it was," buying herself five more minutes to grill Matty Punkin, which was time enough to discover that "boring school" meant "boarding school," that Rod was at one for special kids — for "geniuses, who are also bad, you know, behavior problems" was how Matty described it.

Matty said he didn't know exactly where the school was, only that it was three hours away, and near a farm, and in an area called the "Burpshires." This got a laugh out of Nathaniel, who hooted, "*The Burpshires!*"

The boys broke out in a chorus of burps, and Cass yelled to bring the conversation back to focus. She threatened Matty Punkin, saying he'd be awfully sorry if he was lying. She asked him for Rod's phone number.

"He doesn't have a telephone," Matty told her. "And you can't send him mail — well, you can, but they always read it and tell my parents what's in it. He calls once a week. That's it. Three minutes is all he gets."

"*Burpshires!*" Nathaniel guffawed. The boys started burping again.

Cass had to offer Matty money to pay attention again. After a brief moment of wheeling and dealing, Cass agreed to pay him five dollars to get a message to Rod for her. She wrote it on the back of the hot chocolate receipt:

Meet me at
2 March Hare Road
The Berkshires
The cruelest month
MORE INFO TO COME
                    Signed Levin Not Levine

Later, she'd give Nathaniel another five dollars and a Duncan Imperial to check and make sure Matty had done this. By the time Mrs. Schwartzbaum paid her for babysitting, Cass had already spent the cash and then some. But it was worth it, of course. And Cass would always remember the New York City blizzard as the day her decision turned into a plan.

April is the cruelest month, breeding
Lilacs out of the dead land, mixing
Memory and desire, stirring
Dull roots with spring rain.
Winter kept us warm, covering
Earth in forgetful snow, feeding
A little life with dried tubers.

—T. S. ELIOT
THE WASTE LAND

Chapter Nineteen

Cass spent the next three months in a state of suspense, but she also felt suspended. Funny she'd never connected the words, which were practically the same, but made her feel completely the opposite: nervous and excited whenever she thought about what was going to happen, but also like life was on hold until whatever was going to happen did.

On the day of the blizzard, Cass's decision may have become a plan, but it was a loosely drawn one, based only on a notion that at some point during her week at Timberwood, she'd be returning to the cottage. She didn't know how long she'd stay there — if the key even worked, if she'd go inside. She just knew that at some point she'd be there, and that Rod Punkin would be, too. According to Matty, he'd gotten the message. The kid might have been a liar, but Cass had no choice but to believe him.

If Cass had needed one more sign pointing her in the direction of Rod, her long-ago scheduled appointment with the "brilliant specialist in adolescent issues" was it. Because the therapist Doris insisted she see turned out to be none other than the guy from the party with the gunky throat, Rod's old therapist.

They'd had four sessions so far, and he'd turned out to be an okay guy, though he wouldn't divulge anything about Rod. Whenever Cass asked about him, Gunky Throat (in her head that became her name for him) cited patient-physician confidentiality and conflict of interest, concepts Cass had heard about from Doris but didn't really buy. All she'd gotten him to say was that he remembered Rod — and fondly.

He did know some interesting things. Like what dreams about sculptures meant. "Sculptures in dreams can indicate you find communication with and connections to others difficult," Gunky Throat told her. "Do you feel this way sometimes, Cass?"

"No," she answered. "Well, maybe."

He was the kind of therapist who talked during sessions — and a lot. Cass appreciated this, though lately he'd been on a kick about how grieving took a long time, which was obviously something she already knew. She told him so every time he brought it up.

"Knowing is different from feeling," Gunky Throat reminded her. "Think of it like ice cream. What's your favorite kind?"

"Strawberry," answered Cass in her most exasperated way.

"Well, you may *know* what strawberry ice cream tastes like. You may even be able to remember how good it tastes — how it feels on your tongue, how the little bits of strawberry get lodged in your teeth. But knowing all that isn't the same as actually tasting the strawberry ice cream, is it? If it were, there'd be a lot more successful dieters out there, wouldn't there?"

For a moment, Cass wondered, *Is Gunky Throat calling me fat?*

"The idea of strawberry ice cream, it's not half as satisfying as tasting the ice cream would be. Do you see what I'm saying, Cass? Knowing that grieving is a long process isn't the same as feeling sad."

He was telling her she needed to feel sad. Now, what kind of advice was that? "Isn't a therapist supposed to make someone feel better?" Cass challenged him.

"Better is a relative term," Gunky Throat said with a cough. "A therapist just wants people to feel."

If April was the cruelest month, Cass wondered what February and March had been. After the shock of the January blizzard, New York City settled into a dank routine of rain and hail that left the sidewalks treacherously slippery, the floors of buses coated in an icy muck, and dampened the spirits of even the cheeriest New Yorkers.

Cherry Warner claimed she'd just about had it. Every time Cass saw her, Cherry said something like "New York is too hard," or "Life's too short for this long a winter. I just don't see the point."

"New York City's the best city in the world, *that's* the point," Tillie reminded her mom. "Plus, it's where I go to school!" When Cherry Warner responded that Santa Fe had schools, too, Tillie stomped off in tears. "I thought you wanted me to have the opportunities you didn't have. But you want to pick the opportunities!" They agreed not to discuss it until after Tillie's bat mitzvah: She was under enough pressure as it was.

Even Bea was having trouble keeping an optimistic front. "It's unrelenting," she moaned to Cass, casting mournful eyes over the sculpture garden. "So colorless." When Bea complained of feeling frostbitten on the inside, Doris suggested she go on vacation, preferably somewhere tropical. Bea resisted, not wanting to leave Cass. But Doris claimed "doctor's orders," and she finally agreed, though she wouldn't go until April, when Cass was at Timberwood.

Although it didn't make her proud, Cass actually felt grateful when she learned Bea would be departing the day before Cass was to leave for Timberwood. To be able to pack without Bea checking in on her every two seconds. To have a night to think about the plan! And something felt right about Doris being the one to drive her to school to catch the bus.

We took them to the airport in her blue car. There was a rip in the backseat. My dad let me sit in his lap. I was so short then.

Penelope came over early that evening to say good-bye to Cass.

"Do you want to make sure you have everything you need?" she asked. Penelope prided herself on being an expert packer.

Cass said she had everything.

"I can't believe you haven't tried that outfit on yet," Penelope said, looking across the room at the package from Betsey Johnson. "I bet it would look so good on you! Now that you're wearing those combat boots — you'll be kinda punk rock but kinda not." *A punk rock Beatle,* Cass recalled Rod saying. Then Doris called up from downstairs to ask if Cass wanted pizza for her last meal.

When she got back from dinner, before going to sleep, Cass opened the box from Betsey Johnson, removed the black top, the skirt, and the red tights, thought about trying them on, decided against it, then threw them into the duffel bag she was taking to Timberwood — she had no idea why.

Chapter Twenty

Timberwood wasn't as bad as everyone said it was, and by everyone Cass meant Tillie and Penelope, who'd returned from their weeklong excursion with hideous tales of nature at its foulest. Tillie had contracted a fungus on her foot. Penelope had five spider bites on the back of her neck. "It's a trick!" she told Cass. "I would have given anything to be doing homework instead of hiking in the freezing cold."

For Cass, every activity — the river walk, the rock climb, the trip to the local dairy farm — was a search for something familiar. Was that the apple farm where she'd gotten the cider doughnuts with her mom? Was that the diner where her dad had taken her to breakfast?

At night, she studied the map from the cottage scrapbook, tracing her finger along the fading lines. *Two rights, one left, go across a creek, then straight for one mile.* She'd planned her visit for the fourth day, when Ms. Glitch would be taking the class on an overnight hike. She'd given the information to Matty Punkin, and made him swear a thousand times over he'd relayed it to Rod. She only hoped he wasn't lying.

It was funny to think that of everybody on earth, weird little Matty Punkin was the only person who knew what Cass and Rod were going to do. If anyone else had an inkling, it was Nathaniel — but a bonus limited-edition Duncan Jewel yo-yo had bought Cass his silence, she was pretty sure.

On the third day, with less than twenty-four hours until the plan officially began, Cass had a moment of thinking someone else knew. "I bet you wish your boyfriend was here," Annabella Blumberg remarked. They'd just eaten dinner — Cass's last meal at Timberwood — and were walking back to the cabin.

"What do you mean?" Cass asked with a shudder.

"I mean Rob," Annabella said with a sniff.

Cass was pretty sure she meant Rod. She didn't bother to correct her.

"That kid was a weirdo, but he really made me look good in *Olivia Twisted.*"

Cass couldn't decipher whether Annabella had just given Rod a compliment; still, it was the kindest thing Cass had ever heard her say.

Country sleeping was different from city sleeping, and that night, after plotting her journey, Cass found herself blinking into the darkness, wondering how it could possibly be that tiny little crickets had such big voices. The hours were passing. She had a big morning ahead of her. *I have to sleep!* she told herself. *Sleep!*

Cass had picked an upper bunk in the center of the room. From her vantage point, she could see every bed. She checked to see that her classmates' eyes were closed, and then, when she was absolutely sure there was no chance anyone could hear her, she tucked her head under her blanket and whispered the rhymes:

> *I love you more than a hummingbird sings.*
> *I love you more than butterfly wings.*

Cass fell asleep, but it was a jagged half-sleep, easily interrupted by the wind knocking against the window and Lillian Lang grinding her teeth. She did the rhymes again.

> *I love you more than the stars in the sky.*
> *I love you more than chicken potpie.*

There were no curtains on the windows, so as soon as the sun came up, the cabin filled with light. But the wool blanket was dark and thick, and hidden underneath it, Cass didn't realize it was morning already.

> *We could rhyme until the end of time*
> *About the many ways that you're sublime,*
> *But now we have to go to bed*

So close your eyes, relax your head.
You'll sleep until it's time to wake
And dream of all the rhymes we'll make.

Then Cass heard sounds that weren't crickets, and emerged from underneath the blanket to ten sets of awful eyes blazing before her. They were giving her the looks! Terrible sorry-for-you looks, one enormous pity party.

"I was just talking in my sleep. What's the big deal?" she grumbled, her only consolation knowing that in an hour she'd be gone.

"Okay, I'm going to take one last roll call before we embark on our journey!" said Ms. Glitch. "Does everyone have a canteen? Is it filled? Okay, here goes. "Blumberg, Annabella?"

"Here."

"Chernovsky, Richie?"

"Here."

She kept going.

"Levin, Cass?"

"Here."

But not for long . . .

Chapter Twenty-one

Cass's knapsack bounced against her lower back as she tore across the field. Her canteen was heavy on her shoulder, and she regretted filling it like Ms. Glitch had said to, because it made loud *glub-glub* sounds. For the first half-mile, when she was still on Timberwood property, she was scared someone might hear.

She took the right, and then the other right. She missed the left, and had to double back. Her hair snagged on a branch along the creek, and she nearly slipped on a mossy stone. *What if I fall in? What if I break my leg?* Why hadn't she worried about this before? For days, the staff at Timberwood had been calling the students "city kids." *Is it because I'm a city kid that I didn't worry? Am I a city kid? Is that all I am?*

But Cass made it across without injuring herself too badly, and then a funny thing happened once she was on the other side. Cass was no longer searching for something familiar — everything suddenly was. The poison berry bushes, the smell of a hot dirt road, the sound of cows chewing grass. She stopped thinking about the map; now memory was her guide.

A song was going through her head. Cass didn't know where she'd heard it before, but it made her happy. *"I'm sticking with you / 'Cause I'm made out of glue. / Anything that you might do / I'm gonna do, too!"* went the song.

Cass's sneakers were waterlogged from the creek. They squished as she picked up her step. *"Saw you hanging from a tree / And I made believe it was me! / I'm sticking with you / 'Cause I'm made out of glue!"* And then Cass started to run. She didn't stop until she'd reached March Hare Road.

Cass was tall enough to see over the fence, but she climbed onto the second rung just as she had as a kid. Could these be the same cows? "Hefty, is that you?" she asked an orange one with a yellow bell around its neck. "Sasha, the last time I saw you, you were a calf!" These had to be the same cows, because they still didn't know their names.

Cass hopped off the fence and picked up her stuff, then turned to face the cottage. It was smaller than she remembered and the porch looked more rickety. Had it always been yellow? Cass remembered it being white. There were shades on the windows — Cass remembered purple-and-orange curtains — and then it struck her that she didn't even know if someone lived in the cottage now. Another detail she hadn't thought to think about until now! She crossed the front lawn where she'd looked for slugs. It was sun-splotched and covered in dandelions, and Cass remembered how when she was a kid, she couldn't understand why dandelions were weeds, not flowers. She still couldn't understand.

She was wearing the key around her neck. Standing in front of the closed cottage door, staring at the crooked #2, she felt her skin get hot; she could actually feel the cold key against her collarbone.

This is why I'm here! This is where I'm supposed to be. What's stopping me?

"It's already open," said a voice behind her. "I went in. The place is totally abandoned."

How long had Rod Punkin been standing behind her?

How funny to have all these things to say, and all the time in the world to say them! Sitting on the porch with Rod — they didn't go inside, not just yet — Cass forgot about everybody and everything except how Rod looked the same but sounded different. He sounded quiet when he talked.

"It's called the Mount Academy, and at first all I wanted to do was get back to the city. Winter was super-harsh, you know?" Cass said she did. "But then I got used to it. It's kind of nice to be at a place where everyone's like you."

"You mean behavior problems?" she asked. "You mean like us?"

"Yeah, like us." He was smiling at her. Even Rod's grin seemed quieter. *Can a grin get quieter?* "But, really more like me."

"Hey!" Cass interjected. She might not be the behavior problem Rod was. She'd never been in trouble, after all. But look at her now! Thinking this, she realized that was another thing she hadn't thought about. *Am I in trouble?*

"It's not an insult!"

"I know, but you sound like you like it."

"It's still school; we still have to take Geometry." He sounded almost as if he were consoling her when he said this.

Do I need consoling? wondered Cass. *Do I sound disappointed?*

"But, I don't have to live with my parents. Have you ever noticed that sometimes the wrong people become parents? I swear, if Matty's smart, he'll get out of there, too."

"I thought you'd need to escape," Cass told him. She stared at the floor. There were blades of grass growing in between the warped wooden slats.

"I thought *you* did. Cass, that's why I'm here."

How funny her name sounded in his voice!

"So, what is this place, anyway? Where are we?" Cass explained. "Well, are you gonna show me around or what?" Rod wanted to know.

A lukewarm morning had turned into a hot day. Cass's jeans were caked with mud. At some point, her sweatshirt had ripped, and her sneakers smelled like the creek.

"Do you mind if I change first?" she asked.

Cass went inside the house alone. The bathroom where Bea had kept her lilac perfume and lavender lotion now smelled of mildew. The mirror was scratched and foggy in the way that old glass gets, so Cass could barely see herself. She wasn't sure she wanted to.

She balanced herself on the tub, then struggled to untie the soggy laces of her sneakers. She had to be careful taking off her socks, which were covered in thorns. She peeled off her jeans one leg at a time. There was a long thin cut on her right thigh, the skin on her left knee looked shredded, and her ankles were lined with scratches.

She did her best to get the brambles out of her hair, which, despite being stick straight, had somehow gotten tangled. Cass thought she'd wet it, but when she turned on the faucet, the pipes emitted a gargantuan groan and a spray of dirt. She used the water from her canteen, though it was practically boiling and smelled like plastic.

Cass's knapsack had gotten muddy, but she was relieved to see that the clothes inside were still clean.

She hadn't brought many, the boots took up too much room. Pulling the shirt over her head, she remembered how she'd never tried it on before. But it fit, as far as Cass could tell at least, and so did the skirt.

"Wow," said Rod when she came back outside. "I especially like the boots."

She showed him the place where the garden used to be. She introduced him to the cows. She showed him the lake. She wanted to dunk her feet, but she was wearing tights — so she ran behind a tree and took them off. She threw her combat boots next to his, then joined him on the rock.

Now it was Rod's turn to ask questions. He asked about school, if the class had liked *Olivia Twisted*. He asked how she'd met Matty.

She told him about Ms. Glitch and Timberwood. She told him that Annabella said she missed him and that Lillian Lang wore a nightbrace. She told him about seeing Gunky Throat. She even told him about what had happened that morning, thinking as the words left her mouth: *Was that really only this morning?*

"Oh, come on!" Rod scooped up some lake water in his hand, then used his finger to flick some on her face. "You like having everyone look at you! What about those sunglasses?"

"This is different!" Cass argued.

"So, are you upset that people think you're crazy, or are you scared you really are?"

Cass said she didn't know the answer.

"You're not. Trust me," said Rod. "But you know what might make you feel better?"

"What?"

"Do it out loud. For me."

"Ha!" Cass snorted. She skimmed the tip of her toe along a slimy rock.

"Seriously, sometimes we say stuff out loud by mistake, because it needs to get out. I should know. I'm a world-class psycho, after all." When Rod got desperate, he grinned in the crazy way she remembered. "Come on, what have you got to lose?"

Nothing, Cass thought. *I have nothing left to lose.* And so she said the rhymes to Rod, to the lake, and to all of March Hare Road. When she finished — "You'll sleep until it's time to wake / And dream of all the rhymes we'll make" — she heard her voice replaced by the faint jangling of cowbells.

"Let's try to do one together," Rod suggested when she was finished. "You're not going to make fun of me if I suck, right? Okay, here goes." Rod took a deep breath. "I love you more than the Rolling Stones."

"I love you more than a dog likes bones."

"Hey!" Rod whooped. "Okay, here's another. I love you more than a dinosaur skeleton."

"I love you more than Jell-O-brand gelatin."

They went on like this for a while.

The hot afternoon had turned into a brisk evening, and soon Rod told her that he had to get back before dinner. "I can't get kicked out of this school, too," he said, staring into the frothy gray water. "I can't go home."

Then Cass had a thought that made her happy and sad at once. It was: *Rod's where he's supposed to be.* They put their boots on to walk back. The sun was sinking into the mountains.

"You can come back with me for dinner," Rod offered. "The food's not so bad. We could call Ms. Glitch from there."

This was another part of the plan Cass hadn't thought about. But when they turned onto March Hare Road, she realized she didn't need to. Rod and Cass stood blinking into the glare of twenty bright headlights illuminating the cottage.

Chapter Twenty-two

"I'm sorry. I have to leave," Rod said, sounding nervous. "We have to say good-bye quick."

They were facing each other, but Cass was looking at the ground. The chalky tips of their matching boots almost touched. "You go first," he whispered.

Cass could hear crickets. She felt hungry. "I love you more than beef lo mein," she said to Rod Punkin's shoes.

She felt a hand on her arm, and his voice in her ear. "I love you more than I'm insane."

And then the only boots she was staring at were her own. *I love you more than pumpernickel rye,* she thought as she turned to face the lights. *I love you more than I can cry.*

There were police cars. There was a fire truck. Ms. Glitch was there, so was Doris. "Bea had a hunch you'd be here. Oh, thank goodness she was right! You know, she had to get on a plane, not knowing whether you were dead or alive!" Doris sobbed. "Oh, Cass, how could you be so cruel?"

She barely made it to the porch before she crumpled into Doris's arms.

"I don't know." Cass gulped. "I don't know!"

There were all these sounds around her. There was a siren, voices talking into walkie-talkies. "We've got her," an official voice said.

"She's okay, she's okay!" Ms. Glitch moaned. Cass could barely hear them over Doris's hulking sobs and the song in her head. It was back again, but Cass remembered where she'd heard it.

We were in the car, coming from the cottage, going to Doris's house in the city. "I don't want you to go away," I cried. "Don't go!"

My mom was sitting next to me. I shoved my nose into her shoulder. She was wearing a jean jacket. There was a Peace button on one pocket.

"Why, Cass, this isn't like you!" my mom said. "I spend my life running after you. And now you don't want us to leave? What happened to my little Ms. Independent?"

"Let's sing a song," my dad said. "I'll teach you a new one. It's a silly one with rhymes."

"You love rhymes, Cass!" my mom reminded me.

Now Cass heard her dad's voice, she heard her mom's voice, she heard the little version of her own.

I'll do anything for you, went the song. *Anything you want me to!* Now, sobbing into the folds of Doris's jacket, everything felt familiar — and not in a good way.

"Cass, there was an accident," Doris told me. "They were

in a car. It crashed." Anything you want me to, went the song. *"They're dead." I'm sticking with you. . . .*

"There was an accident, Cass. It's your parents, Cass."

Well, it had sounded preposterous, like Dr. Seuss or a Mad Lib, like when little kids mix words that don't go together and think it's a riot. Like: electronic giraffe doorknob. Or oatmeal tree butt. It had sounded so absurd, Cass had almost laughed. *My parents died and I almost laughed.* Cass's body shook, remembering this. *"I'm sorry!"* she wailed. *"I'm sorry!"*

"It's okay," Doris said, touching her hair. "Cass, it's going to be okay."

One by one, the police cars left. Ms. Glitch told Doris she had to get back; she'd check in with her tomorrow.

"It's cold, Cass. Do you want to go inside?" Doris asked her once they were alone. "I don't have my key, but we never locked this place." Cass said no, thinking one trip inside had been enough — without the people who'd once lived there, the cottage wasn't really the cottage anymore. "Are you sure? Well, okay, she'll be here soon, anyway."

The crickets were out in full force, but Cass still found a way to sleep. Wrapped in a blanket left by a policeman, her head in Doris's large lap, waiting for Bea, Cass was hit with a lulling sense of relief. *All this time,* she'd wondered. *Somewhere, somehow, could I have known?* Now Cass knew — *I didn't know* — and fell asleep.

"Sometimes the wrong people become parents," Rod had said.

Cass woke up to the sound of Sylvia Hempel barking. Oh, she was glad Bea had company for the ride! Doris was snoring next to her. "They're here," she said, shaking her aunt's arm. "Bea's here!" Cass tore off the blanket and streaked across the driveway to hug Bea, thinking, *But sometimes the right people become parents, too.*

Chapter Twenty-three

"So, Rod Punkin is your boyfriend," said Penelope, once she'd gotten home and told them everything.

"No," said Cass. "I don't even know when I'll see him again. If I will —"

"You will," Tillie assured her.

It had been a lot of work, telling her friends everything. They'd had to have a sleepover, and then they'd had to extend it a night. They'd pulled Cass's mattress onto the floor and put the guest cots next to it. "It's a bed floor!" Cass had yelped. "Maybe I'll keep it like this forever!"

"You'll have to clean up your room before Bea agrees to that." Penelope laughed.

Cass ignored this. "Why do you think most beds are rectangles? I think beds should come in all kinds of shapes, like circles and trapezoids, and maybe even parallelograms!" In Geometry, they were studying quadrilaterals now. "Do you think I'd make a million dollars if I invented the parallelogram bed?!"

"What about a triangle bed?" Tillie wondered.

Cass said she guessed it could work if you slept with the pointy part at your feet, but that wouldn't work if you had a dog. And Cass needed room at the foot of her bed for Sylvia Hempel, who'd returned to Cass's room — at least for part of the night. Cass wasn't sure when in the night the dog arrived; all she knew was she went to sleep by herself, but woke with Sylvia Hempel there.

It dawned on Cass that maybe the dog had been dividing her nights for a while now — and that if she'd come and gone while Cass was sleeping, Cass would never have known. But that was the funny thing about feeling left out. Once Cass stopped feeling left out, she stopped leaving people out, which made her wonder if she'd ever actually been left out!

It turned out that as much as Cass had to tell Penelope and Tillie, they had to tell her. Tillie's Torah and haftorah portions had gone off without a hitch, but the party had been a total disaster. Tillie's father had insisted his girlfriend do a blessing for the bread with him, then the girlfriend had forgotten her lines, and Cherry was forced to fill in. Someone had turned up the temperature in the synagogue basement, melting the frosting on Tillie's cake, turning the peace sign into a gooey scribble-scrabble swirl. Tillie even had snapshots. "It looks like Bea's modern art!" Cass exclaimed when Tillie showed her the picture. "That's a good thing!"

Apparently, Cherry Warner was still on her moving kick. Tillie had started to calm down about it. "I'm switching tactics. If I can't convince her not to move, I can at least get her to compromise. Would you guys visit me if I move to San Francisco? What about Los Angeles?"

Meanwhile, Penelope had started talking on the phone to a kid from two of her classes. "The guy's a mute," Tillie reported. "We've had French and Ancient Civilization with him all year, and he never says a word in either. But these guys talk for hours every night."

"I guess you could say he's kinda psycho," Penelope said with a shrug.

"Maybe we all are a little bit," Cass replied.

In Cass's case, it turned out Rod had been right — Cass wasn't a behavior problem after all. Her Timberwood escapade hadn't even gotten her suspended. Apparently Elston Prep only cared about behavior problems when they affected grades. Cass had affected a daylong hike. All Cass had to do was agree to visit Gunky Throat twice a week. She didn't see this as a punishment — Gunky Throat could be pretty smart sometimes, and being in his office made Cass feel close to Rod. Hanging out with Matty Punkin every now and then did, too. "If Matty's smart, he'll get out of there, too," Rod had said. But Cass wanted to look out for him while he was still around.

After Ms. Glitch's English class returned from

Timberwood, the teacher announced they'd be disbanding discussion groups and moving on to independent studies. She gave them a list of novels to choose from.

Cass picked Charles Dickens's *Great Expectations.* It was the only book on the list about an orphan, and she wanted to give it a chance.

.

WORDS YOU THINK AREN'T REAL WORDS
but REALLY ARE
(check your dictionary — SWEAR!)

Muck-a-muck

Humongous

Splendiferous

Crackpot

Hotfoot

Gonzo

Fluky

Lickety-split

Rhinotillexomania ← LOOK THAT UP!
YOU'LL CRACK UP!
SWEAR!

Lollygag

Hothead

Imbecilic

youR (whoeveR you ARe!) peRSonal FavoRite woRdS

1.

2.

3.

4.

5.

6.

7.

8.

9.

10.

TO FIND OUT MORE ABOUT CASS

AND HER FRIENDS, VISIT

WWW.ALISONPOLLET.COM.